FRIENDS AT WATERS-EDGE
AND FREMONT HOUSE

FRIENDS AT WATERS-EDGE AND FREMONT HOUSE

MARGARET MARGERESON

Matador
Unit E2 Airfield Business Park,
Harrison Road, Market Harborough,
Leicestershire. LE16 7UL
Tel: 0116 279 2299
Email: books@troubador.co.uk
Web: www.troubador.co.uk/matador
Twitter: @matadorbooks

ISBN 978 1 80313 279 2

British Library Cataloguing in Publication Data.
A catalogue record for this book is available from the British Library.

Printed and bound in the UK by TJ Books Limited, Padstow, Cornwall
Typeset in 11pt Minion Pro by Troubador Publishing Ltd, Leicester, UK

Matador is an imprint of Troubador Publishing Ltd

It gives me great pleasure to write the dedication to my dear late wife's book. This is the fulfilment of Margaret's ambition to have her book published and tell you her story. I hope it brings you, the reader, as much joy reading her story as I know Margaret had writing it.

I should like to thank friends and the publishing team for their help in enabling me to realise Margaret's wish.

An Introduction:
Bizarre Events with Mysterious Results

After the sudden onset of the mysterious illness that had attacked his immune system and devastated his body, Matthew Weldon had been flown home by air ambulance from Revalian and immediately admitted to Mountfield Hospital. Now, after ten long tedious months, he was being discharged. It had not been possible for the medical scientists to exactly identify the pernicious virus responsible, but the cocktail of antibiotics and carefully orchestrated medical attention had gradually sorted him out, at least partially, although he still suffered periods of extreme exhaustion, a condition which he had been told was not likely to vanish any time soon.

The conference trip had certainly left its mark. He was particularly aggrieved as he had only volunteered to stand in for a colleague who had been unable to attend due to a persistent personal problem, and now looking back he rather wished he hadn't been so helpful.

Taking account of all the negative predictions and

probabilities concerning his illness, it was surprising that he was still alive!

Having been resident at the hospital for such a prolonged period he had become something of a permanent occupant which had led medical staff to wave him off with fond farewells as he walked towards the privately hired car that had been sent, courtesy of his company, to take him home. It had stopped conveniently at the bottom of the wide stone steps to pick him up, but he soon realised just how weak and inflexible his limbs had become as he slowly stooped forward to get into the vehicle, which was not designed to cater for the transportation of the less mobile.

Once Matthew had regained consciousness, he had been transferred from intensive care onto a hospital ward. His mind, though, was still full of the characters who had been his constant companions throughout his devastating illness. He had been an enthusiastic onlooker into their world and each day, as he watched the events of their life unfold in his mind's eye, he had been given the will to live; without that connection he felt he would have given up and expired. The doctors explained that when patients were in a coma and as ill as he had been the strong concoction of prescribed drugs that have to be administered play bizarre tricks on the mind, often leading to vivid and realistic dreams, sometimes psychedelic episodes.

Matt knew that this must be true. There was, though, no doubt in his mind that he had experienced something uniquely different. The daily sequence of events that he had witnessed when he had been unconscious were no less vivid to him now than they were before, when he had been at death's door. The memories were crystal clear; they never faded with time nor became less important to him in the way that dreams or psychological meanderings invariably do in the end, however profound.

An explanation existed, but how could Matthew have been aware that experimental motion threads of free animated organisms had been set free by researchers functioning in a sphere in an alien environment, millions of light years away from Earth? Travelling far beyond their terrain in the most northerly extremities of the isolated galactic outreaches and the inner sections of the Milky Way (which leads to the vast hazy nebulae on the other side) these moving organisms, containing the genetic material of fictional characters capable of independent dynamic activity and free will, were instructed by their perceptive masters, Kettlebaston, Meynell and Jasper, to seek out and program the brain of a ripe and helpless earthling in order to try out the first of their novel experiments and to implant this initial dynamic activity. All they needed for the trial to allow the experimenters to chart and record the outcome of the experiment was the psyche of the host target. A donor such as Matt in a weakened psychological and physiological medical state was ideal. And so the experiment was well and truly underway.

Kettlebaston, Meynell and Jasper had studied life on Earth in great detail and their plan, however long it took, was to manipulate earthly existence and to steal its resources. Their vision of building up a bank of vulnerable earthlings to control, manipulate and use as strategic stepping stones now seemed to be within their grasp, or so they hoped.

The experimenters had assumed that the memory of this first experiment would deteriorate once the earthling had regained consciousness, but this part of their plan had not gone quite to book. It turned out that the experimental activity could not be neutralised and destroyed as predicted and could perhaps even take on a hitherto unexpected and distorted dimension.

The scary truth is that we never know who or what is watching and using us, nor are we aware of how complicated a mesh we could each unwittingly become a part of.

After Matt arrived home from the hospital, it had taken him a week or so to settle back into some kind of basic routine. One morning he felt determined that he must try harder to achieve a daily achievement of some kind, and so he decided to start up his laptop and to begin typing out his first batch of reminiscences, starting from the time when he had been so near to death in the intensive care unit. It was not like creating a story: he had no plot or characters to invent as it was all there for him as a documentary in his mind.

He had no intention of doing anything in particular with his draft: his reminiscences only resulted from a need to put down a clear record of events for his own peace of mind and to give himself something to concentrate on during the long recuperation process which he still had to endure. He had been told that it would be very many weeks or perhaps months before he could return to work.

Flowing from his fingertips and onto the keyboard his reflections took their shape and so this is how the peculiar story went.

A Brief Background

The rabbits that inhabited the Ultor Commune were called Ultorians: they were also referred to as Ultorian Scoodles, a derogatory nickname given to them by members of the Challion Community (a rival rabbit settlement that existed nearby).

Senior Ultorians were called Ultorian Elderians and the Chief Elderian went by the name of Mould.

Rilganna was a Beveranian, a large Blue Beveren rabbit with thick lavender-coloured fur who lived at the Ultor Commune; treated indifferently and dismissed as an outsider, she was the only one of her kind within the local communities.

1

Rilganna's Premonition and Her Unenviable Situation at the Ultor Commune

Rilganna could tell that big trouble was brewing in the commune: the atmosphere had changed, and life felt more unpredictable than usual. Her ears developed an involuntary twitch and instinct told her to be wary.

There was a sudden instability beneath her paws. This was followed by a disturbing shudder; it came from nowhere and was like being on board ship when the sea was very bumpy. At first she was startled, but had no time to spend working out what was causing this new phenomenon, for just at the moment it was the least of her problems, her mind being distracted by other more serious things.

She knew she only had herself to blame for the mess she found herself in. Earlier that morning, as she tried to make friends with a group of rabbits, inhabitants from the

Challion Community, she noticed a few Elderians staring straight at her from behind the tall spiral tree on the edge of the clearing in the bluebell wood. Her activity had made them very angry as there were many outstanding disputes between the two rival clans and bitterness had been steadily worsening between them for some time.

Having no other option, she carried on with her normal routine, running errands throughout the day, but as she frequented the dim candle-lit tunnels Rilganna started to become aware of an ominous sign – a ball of black rolling dust with a staring bright green eye fixed in its centre was quivering and hovering in the foreground; it was making its existence visible to her whichever way she turned. This well-known precursor for the presence of evil did nothing to settle her uneasy mind.

It was late in the afternoon when Rilganna's attention was drawn to the small gathering of Elderians huddled close together in the commune; they were lurking near the damp murky corner where the two main passages crossed. The recent heavy downpour had added strength to a persistent water leak that had dripped through a narrow crack in the low dank roof for months. Now it had turned into a persistent flow of dirty water which was forcing its way through the thick mass of accumulated black cobwebs. Every now and again filthy water splashed onto their mean little faces, but the Elderians were too engrossed in their secretive whispers and menacing glances aimed towards Rilganna to notice any discomfort.

When it was time for her to go to bed, Rilganna's fear was incalculable, and determined though she was to remain watchful as the shadows of night-time closed in, her eyes grew heavier and heavier and finally her resolve was overridden and she was seduced by the sweet call of sleep. It was during that fateful night that she suddenly awoke to find two of the most spiteful Elderians pulling her up from her truckle bed. At the speed of light she was pushed into an old carrot sack that was then dragged along the ground and thrown into the back of the rickety cart, left as it always was near to the commune entrance.

The decaying wagon, with the remnants of peeling blue paint barely clinging to its surface, started to move forward; it jolted and wobbled along the deep track leading away from the Ultor Commune, one of many dug out from the grassy hillsides. In the low land at the bottom of the hills, the sludge and silt resulting from the recent torrential rain had created piles of thick wet mud on the ground; this always happened between the turn of the autumn and winter season. She listened intently as the wagon's wheels splashed noisily through the sodden earth. In this neighbourhood there had always been little inter-activity and even less conviviality between the two main divergent clans who had lived cheek by jowl in this remote district for generations, just about tolerating each other's presence.

During that desolate journey shock and fear took hold of Rilganna and she began to inhabit a world of her own, allowing fanciful memories to play on in her mind. Predicting that her life was about to end, she started to reminisce, muttering in a despondent kind of way.

'How I shall miss seeing the sun rise in the morning, and later in the day watching the bees hover in the still hot air. I so enjoyed sitting in the top field on long summer nights under the spreading sycamore tree near to the deep lily pond…'

At this moment her reflections became of little importance for she had noticed that the rickety old cart had suddenly pulled up to a halt.

Rilganna listened closely and after a short pause she heard a series of muffled sounds and the movement of hobnailed boots scraping on the ground. Suddenly the old carrot sack was grabbed, and she felt herself being unceremoniously tipped out onto the kerbside of the hard stony highway with only a small bag of meagre possessions and her old brown winter coat, both of which followed her as the contents of the sack were emptied.

'We are rid of her now and see how she likes that. Perhaps one of those rabbits from the Challion Community she's always trying to befriend will come to her rescue!' she heard Mould, the Chief Elderian, say in a loud and hostile manner.

He was sneering, sniggering and hissing in a mean way and the other Elderians were joining in as the dilapidated old wagon, having been turned round on its wheels, began to make its way back to the commune; gradually the taunting and the raucous utterances emanating from her tormentors disappeared from earshot.

Rilganna was disorientated after this cruel ordeal and for a short time she remained static and motionless, like the dead weight of a fallen statue, hardly daring to move. The awkward landing had caused her legs to graze and be sore and she felt bruised all over but eventually she found her energy and struggled onto the pavement from the kerbside, shivering against the chill night air. With her heart beating fiercely in her chest and hardly being able to take a breath, she began to take stock of her situation.

She peered through the low light of the infrequent street lamps, desperately looking for a sign to give her some comfort, but all she saw was a line of formidable-looking houses sturdily built with tall red brick chimneys, set in their own substantial grounds with each window robed in tightly drawn curtains or blinds. Rilganna knew that the position she was now in was not without its dangers; she was vulnerable, hanging about motionless and friendless in an unknown place, and she had to make a move.

We never know who is watching us and so it was for Rilganna. She was completely unaware that her every move was being scrutinised from behind a thick hedge by a curious and apprehensive Zig-Zag Pontoon, who was a small robot. He was himself in the middle of a mind-blowing crisis and could not see his desperate situation coming to a happy conclusion any time soon. Feeling down in the dumps and being a robot without any feasible plan to get himself out of his predicament he had just been standing there staring through a gap in the tightly packed twigs of the dusty hedge, pondering on his grim prospects.

By now Rilganna had managed to put on and button up her worn-out and skimpy coat as best she could as the sleeves were too short and tight making the activity difficult; this saved her from carrying it and its meagre warmth gave her a crumb of comfort. She picked up her linen bag and began to make her way along the street. Meanwhile, curiosity and the desire not to be completely alone got the better of Zig-Zag Pontoon and so on the spur of the moment he hastily left the safety of the high hedge and began following Rilganna.

Having made slow progress she came across a narrow turning off to the left that led from the main street into a quiet narrow lane. She faltered, checked all about her, and then decided to change direction as it occurred to her that this dimly lit byroad might be a safer place for her to be. As

Rilganna turned, Zig-Zag did the same, while keeping a good clear distance from her so that he wasn't spotted.

Zig-Zag had been produced in a massive robotics factory, which was located in remote countryside, a few miles north of Landsmoth. He was put together in a hurry because of a sudden surge in orders that had been received at the Works. He was one among hundreds of small robots that had been programmed to do gardening and general do-it-yourself jobs. He was shortly to be parcelled up in a box to be posted from the factory's despatch department to just about anywhere on planet Earth, depending on his fate. Well, let's be honest, who wants to be regarded as a program to be sold on to do someone else's jobs and to get no reward or appreciation for doing it?

Zig-Zag was not like the other robots on the production line, who just accepted their lot. This was because a trial chip had been placed inside his workings which enabled him to have the benefit of an experimental run of "artificial intelligence". The AI chip was scheduled for removal, but the researcher forgot to take it out, which was good news for Zig-Zag Pontoon who made sure that no one noticed anything different about his behaviour from the other robots.

The ability of Zig-Zag to think for himself had enabled him to watch out for a chance to plan his escape, and one Tuesday morning he saw his route to freedom. The group controller had been careless, and a door had been left ajar and so Zig-Zag Pontoon grabbed his battery, plug and cable and zig-zagged out through the gap and clattered round to the back of the premises during a staff tea break. There he squatted down and hid behind a tall rubbish bin until everyone at the factory had gone home. He had got away with it, and no one had missed him. He knew, though, that he had to move quickly to get himself to somewhere that had an accessible electrical power socket as he needed to get plugged in and charged up in order to keep his intellect processing.

Eventually, finding that the way was all clear, he clattered away from the factory grounds and, seeing some bright neon signs flashing on the outside of a garage-cum-convenience-store across the road, he decided to go for it and to zig-zag over the busy highway. He had a couple of near misses as heavy trucks thundered past him, almost knocking him for six, but he made it to the other side and managed to sneak through the door of the busy filling station as a customer laden with newly purchased goods came out.

In the corner of the convenience store he saw an electrical power socket low down on the wall near the cheese, milk and yogurt cold store. He zig-zagged over, plugged his battery into the socket and pushed the small plug, which was on the other end of the cable, into the robotic socket on his left arm. In fact, no one took any notice of him as he looked like any one of the many robotic staff industriously jiggling away and tidying the various products that filled the refrigerated area; these days the sight of a working robot hardly turned a hair on anyone's head.

Once Zig-Zag was sufficiently charged up, and the coast was all clear, he got going again: he made his exit from the filling station store as soon as he saw an opportunity and hurriedly clattered along the street. He saw a bus coming along and so he joined the end of the queue at the bus stop. It was a bit of a push, but he struggled on board and stood on the platform just inside the open entrance so that he could get off quickly if he needed to. This happened sooner rather than later; a fare-checker was coming along to make sure everyone had a valid authority to travel as there had been some fare dodging of late, which was about to be clamped down upon, so Zig-Zag rapidly rang the bell and managed to hasten off the vehicle without paying.

It was just as well that he made his escape as he certainly didn't want to draw any attention to himself or to have to answer any awkward questions. In addition to which he had no robotic currency, or any other kind of currency for that matter, and he certainly didn't have one of those lobster card things that he had recently heard about. Once off the bus Zig-Zag hid behind a thick hedge, which was where he was stationed when he first caught sight of Rilganna being roughly dumped onto the roadside from the old carrot sack.

Rilganna was making good progress and Zig-Zag was still following her. She found the perimeter of the narrow lane to be lined by well-stocked gardens on both sides with tall trees growing intermittently along the way, their bulky overhanging branches creating a reassuring archway. She was searching for a sheltered hedge or a leafy nook where she could sleep out the night in relative safety. As she followed the gently curving right-hand bend she saw a rambling Victorian-style house on the left-hand side, with a long sweeping driveway leading to a sizeable porch with an elegant portico framing a substantial front door. The approach to the property was complemented by two immaculately manicured lawns which were divided by small neatly trimmed trees and bushes, the final embellishment being an active garden fountain which splashed blue-coloured water forcefully into the air.

Zig-Zag continued to keep a decent distance from Rilganna, as he didn't want to be seen by her. Even though his robotic world had been one of little experience, he felt sure within himself that following a nervous rabbit, tightly clutching a small linen bag, who appeared to be as lost as he was, did not seem quite the right thing to do. He started to feel guilty, but he had no other hope to cling to and following Rilganna was some kind of consolation, of which he had no intention of letting go.

Rilganna, continuing to look earnestly about her, noticed a tall, detached building standing some distance from the left-hand side of the Victorian residence. It was a kind of summer or garden house and, although unconventional in design, it appeared to be well constructed. Its walls were made up of neatly laid sand-faced Heather brickwork, and it had a tiled hexagonal roof.

With the moon helping to light her path, she slowly made her way across the gravel area that led to the building and approached its crudely constructed door, which as it turned out was not properly secured. All of a sudden, a small beam of light appeared, near the bottom of the old barn door, which helped Rilganna to see more clearly. Puzzled, she looked to her left side and spotted a plump bespectacled man, hardly more than two feet tall, standing close by, watching her.

'Hello, stranger, take my torch. You will need it when you get inside as that building is as dark as coal. When the beam dims and starts to ebb away, push the switch back on again and shake the torch vigorously because that is just how it is.'

Having spoken these instructions, the bespectacled one took a few steps backwards, adopted the appearance of a stoutly sized puffin and then flew off, seemingly to some kind of social function as he was now neatly dressed in a yellow dinner jacket complete with a flattering orange-coloured cravat. Rilganna noticed that a large bunch of yellow roses, which perfectly matched the colour of his dinner jacket, was neatly tucked into a bag hanging down from under one of his wings. The wings had not been visible to Rilganna when the strange little character was standing on the ground next to her and she was temporarily taken aback by the sudden transformation.

'What it is to find a friend even if he was a bit odd,' muttered Rilganna, who could see no new reason to worry about her safety, and in any case, she had nothing to lose, so she cautiously pushed at the door and then with all her strength she gave it more of a shove, and squeezed through the space now made big enough to fit her body. Slowly the beam of the torch dimmed and ebbed away just as the puffin-like character said it would.

Zig-Zag Pontoon had now caught up with Rilganna and was hiding behind some shrubbery in the nearby garden, where he was able to watch what she was doing. He was beginning to grow tired of hiding behind foliage but for the time being that seemed to be his only option. He stared and squinted when Rilganna pushed through the gap in the old door and disappeared inside the building. With all his heart he wanted to be there with her, but he was shy and unsure as to whether Rilganna would like him (robots were not everyone's cup of tea and still aren't) so he took the easy option and stayed where he was.

Meanwhile Rilganna was relieved to find some shelter. She began to absorb the unfamiliar surroundings as her eyes moved quickly from one part of the building to the other, focusing on the different aspects that confronted her. Suddenly from a far corner she was aware of a low reverberating moan, which was immediately followed by an eerie silence. Rilganna waited to see whether any further manifestation was about to develop but nothing more happened. Was it that Rilganna's interruption of the peace had awakened and stirred up some normally silent spirit? She had no explanation and so decided then and there not to start worrying about it, for at the moment she had enough to deal with, and in any case, there was no space left in her mind for anything new.

The substantial structure had a rough and incomplete ground floor and no upper floor; it was in fact a lofty shell of a building, reminiscent of a project that had never properly got off the ground. Feeling reassured that she was as safe as she could expect to be she put down her linen bag in a corner near a neat pile of hay and looked at the few possessions inside it; there was a small thin blanket, some dry stale carrots, and her old brown winter hat.

Sitting alone with the hurt of abandonment as her only companion, the realisation of her situation took hold. Salty tears began to drop down from Rilganna's eyes, eventually dripping off the end of her whiskers. She began to look back and reflect on her life, as anyone in this situation might do. She had always been an outsider in the community network, really belonging nowhere. Trying to socialise with others from the different clans had not been easy. Sometimes they would start to react positively, but they would quickly become wary, clam up and disappear from view when they realised where she came from, as all the residents from the Ultor Commune were considered by others to be social pariahs and this included her.

Rilganna rubbed her eyes with her paws, for she knew she was beginning to feel sorry for herself and this kind of negative attitude did no good at all, so she engaged a well-tried and tested technique for remedying gloomy thoughts, which involved sitting back, crossing her front legs, closing her eyes and visualising a luxuriant green meadow full of delicate white daisies moving with the breeze. She was often puzzled why this technique helped her to find harmony within herself, but it seemed to work.

After this manoeuvre and a deep yawn, she realised how very tired she was and so she covered herself over as best she could with the small grubby blanket she had found in her linen bag and fell fast asleep on the small pile of hay in the corner.

Zig-Zag Pontoon was now outside the door of the old building, feeling worried and utterly miserable: he wanted to get inside but was still not able to work out how to go about it, so he decided to continue hanging around until daybreak in the hope that he might then find the courage to make a move.

When Rilganna woke up, all she could hear at first was the birds singing loudly, but it was not long before the cackling guffaws of the Ultorian Elderians that she had heard the night before, as they shunted off in the old cart, began to reverberate in her mind. At first she was puzzled about where she was; it was not long before all the scary memories gradually came back to her, but something else was now bothering her.

Speaking firmly to herself, she said, 'There's no getting away from it. I must try to get myself sorted and thinking straight. When I arrived here last night there were definitely no stairs installed in the building and therefore no upper floor, and certainly no windows on the ground floor. However, this morning I find a spiral staircase made of strong shiny steel leading to an upper floor; the ground floor now has floorboards; walls painted light blue have created rooms, and windows have appeared; instead of the ill-fitting barn door at the front entrance to the building, a new solid oak door now stands in its place, firmly shut.'

This, though, was not all there was, as near to Rilganna's linen bag there was a polished front door key threaded onto a stainless steel ring by a strong piece of string; an illustrated book full of colourful wild flowers; a flask of hot tea; a large white china dish and mug; a carton of creamy milk and a substantial bag of crunchy cereal, the kind she really enjoyed. The apprehension that she had experienced the night before had all but melted away and in its place was bewilderment, for Rilganna's world was now a deeply puzzling place.

Feeling hungry, she put all the recent strange goings-on out of her mind and concentrated on eating some breakfast and looking through her book. The sun streamed in through the newly created windows, and she felt the gentle winter sun permeating her thick fur.

Zig-Zag Pontoon was now getting desperate. He hadn't slept a wink all night, and as his intellectual workings had remained active his battery was now running down again and he was beginning to feel depressed, addled and unbalanced. His mechanisms were playing up big time, and this was no joking matter. Zig-Zag liked his life, difficult though it was, and he was determined to keep going.

It was no good, he could wait no longer. He struggled along as best he could and went to the closed door of the old building; he banged on it with all the strength he could muster in his small metal arms. Rilganna eventually found the courage to open the door and stared in astonishment at what she saw.

'Please can I plug myself in somewhere?' Zig-Zag Pontoon blurted out. 'I am at my wits' end and feeling very faint...'

Having said this, Zig-Zag suddenly collapsed with a mighty clatter of metal on the ground right in front of an astonished Rilganna. Acting in haste, and with great difficulty, she pushed and pulled at Zig-Zag until finally she managed to drag him inside the building and over to the only power socket she could see, and quickly plugged him in.

'Oh dear, how very odd all this is turning out to be,' said Rilganna, getting more perplexed as each minute went by, and not for the first time speaking out loud to herself. 'I do so hope I haven't lost the plot, as things don't seem to be working at all like they normally do.'

2

Rilganna, Zig-Zag Pontoon and Bardwell

Rilganna kept a watchful eye on the unconscious Zig-Zag Pontoon while he was connected to the power point in the corner. He didn't look very comfortable, so she put her old winter coat under his metal head just in case he suddenly jumped into life and banged it on the floor.

She had finished her breakfast, and as there wasn't much else to do, she sat daydreaming in the corner of the sunny room. She was trying to work out what her next move should be but couldn't think of anything at all that made much sense. She was not long into her considerations before she heard a banging noise on the oak door, which quickly turned her pensiveness into unease; she could hardly believe that this was happening for a second time. Above all she very much hoped that it was not another robotic stranger needing a power point, as she had no idea of the location of a second one and in any case one small robot was quite enough to look out for.

She peered out of the window and her eyes settled on a badger, who had a bulky knapsack on his back, standing near the door. He was a substantial individual from what she could see through the glass. His green woollen tweed coat was in need of a good brush down, and what's more, his boots were very muddy. Rilganna slowly turned the key in the lock of the new oak door and warily looked through the slightly opened edge.

As Rilganna stared curiously at the stranger, he stared back. He removed his oversized cap and in an ill at ease, hesitant kind of way, said, 'I was wondering whether there was any chance of a bite to eat or more than one bite if you can spare it. I have had a long uncomfortable ride in a truck from the city to the countryside and as there was no chance of buying any refreshments along the way I am feeling rather hungry, and thirsty, too.'

He certainly looked tired and a bit sorry for himself and for some reason, and odd though this might seem, Rilganna couldn't think of a good excuse to turn the badger away, for she immediately found him likeable although he had a very funny way of saying things. Anyway, what did it matter; she threw caution to the wind and invited him in. After all, her whole life was now very odd and taking a wider view of things why should she be concerned about the arrival of a badger, and at least he would be a bit of company, which she was rather short of.

Having been invited inside, the badger stepped into the room and took off his muddy boots, leaving them just inside the door, along with his cap and bulky knapsack, which made an unsightly lumpy pile on the floor.

After securing the oak door behind her, Rilganna and the newcomer sat together on the small pile of hay in the corner by the sunlit window, feeling a little awkward with each other, as new acquaintances so often do. After they had exchanged names, Bardwell, with the white china bowl now perched precariously on his lap, ate a large helping of cereal at Rilganna's invitation, and enjoyed two mugs of tea from the flask. After a few sideways glances, and with polite conversation having passed between them, they started to feel more at ease with one another and began to talk openly about their recent experiences. (By the way Bardwell's full name was Hinderlay Bardwell Lucifer Badger but he preferred plain Bardwell: he never mentioned his full name to anyone, as it took too long, and people got bored waiting for the end to come.)

Suddenly Bardwell noticed the heap of plugged-in robot on the floor in the corner but, thinking that it might be considered ill-mannered to make any comment, he just carried on as if this was all quite normal.

Rilganna was puzzled. It seemed odd to her that Bardwell had undertaken an excursion so ill-prepared, with nothing to eat or drink in his knapsack, especially as in general terms he appeared to be an organised kind of character. His knapsack looked full to bursting with something but of course she had no idea what was in it. She gave him her full attention and listened very carefully to what he had to say. As Bardwell got deeply involved in his conversation with Rilganna she noticed that his ears began to glow; gradually they became a good bit brighter than the rest of him, and although she tried very hard, she found it impossible not to stare at them.

'I am afraid that my story of late is not a very cheerful one,' said Bardwell, looking rather dejected, 'for I have fallen into the worst of hard times. I recently lost my job at the investment bank, as it finally closed its doors, being a victim of the financial downturn, and as a consequence I had to vacate my two rented rooms in the large house near the bank where I lived for a long time, because I could no longer pay my rent. I only have a very small amount of cash left, as it has been some months since the bank paid its employees anything like a normal pay packet, and I have been living off my savings ever since, which have now all but vanished.'

It was a fact that due to this hapless situation Bardwell was to all intents and purposes destitute. He was desperate for some kind of new start, finding that the experiences of the past few weeks had rendered him low in spirit and lacking in verve and enthusiasm, so unlike his usual self, and so from the city full of bad memories he had found his way to the small village of Crindling.

Bardwell continued his story, his ears still glowing brightly, for he had the kind of personality that once he started on something he needed to finish it.

'I attracted the attention of a truck driver who was travelling along the main road near my old home. I was pleased that I had successfully thumbed down a vehicle with my paw, or at least I think that's what the manoeuvre is called. The driver was puzzled because I didn't know where I wanted to go, nor did I care, so he discharged me where he was delivering a large box of electrical goods to a big house, which was at the end of this lane. He was worried about how I would manage, but he offered me some good advice about keeping my chin up and, having given me a hearty pat on the back, he helped me out of the cab and waved cheerfully as I stood motionless on the pavement, not quite knowing what to do next.'

Rilganna sympathised with this dilemma, as she knew only too well what it felt like to be all lost at sea while still being on dry land and to be pushed here, there and everywhere by the tide of life, finding it impossible to think of any action that might inject some sense into things that had become completely weird.

When Bardwell had finished talking, Rilganna began to tell him about her life to date, and how all the demanding and repetitive jobs at the Ultor Commune had filled her days. There had been the endless laundry to do, the tidying and sweeping of the residents' rooms, which were deep underground, and then there was all the shopping to do, followed by the cooking, not to mention having to carry out running repairs in the commune when things went wrong. Bardwell was deeply moved by her story and taken aback by the harsh and unfair treatment she had recently experienced at the hands of the Ultorian Elderians.

As the goings-on from the previous night tumbled out from Rilganna like water from a burst pipe, she told Bardwell about the strange noise she heard when she first arrived, and the changes that had occurred in the garden house during the hours of darkness. Bardwell was puzzled and began to wonder whether Rilganna was in a state of shock and muddle, but they decided that under these oddest of circumstances they should cease from too much analysis and wait to see what turned up during the next couple of days.

It was reassuring for Rilganna that Bardwell had arrived, and she felt all the better for having someone to share this new and unpredictable situation with, although of course she didn't know how long he would stay. Bardwell had a calm aspect about him and was the right type of companion to have around while there were so many mysterious events going on.

After Bardwell had finished his breakfast and their explanations were done, they felt more cheerful and so together they decided to venture outdoors, leaving Zig-Zag Pontoon plugged into the power socket as he looked contented enough and his metal bodywork was still looking shiny, which was a good sign. Having locked the oak door behind them, they carefully checked around outside and then started to walk cautiously away from the front gravel. It was not long before they came across a small general store and went inside. It was an old-fashioned type of shop, with the pungent smell of good wholesome food and newly baked bread hanging in the air.

'Look, Rilganna,' said Bardwell, spotting some tasty things, 'you can have some of those big red apples, some cheese and a lettuce to go with it. The food for sale looks so fresh and appetising, and I'll have this lemon drizzle cake; it is my favourite as I have rather a sweet tooth.'

Using most of the money that Bardwell had left in his pocket they bought the goods, but Bardwell couldn't help feeling just a bit guilty that he had been unable to resist the yummy-looking cake, as he knew it was bad for his teeth and he had left his toothbrush and toothpaste behind when he left his flat.

On the way back the helpful badger explained to Rilganna that he had his laptop computer in his knapsack, which was why it looked so tightly packed and overflowing at the seams. Rilganna didn't know a lot about computers, except that some of the Ultorian Scoodles played games on them at the commune, but she was never allowed to join in. Looking over their heads, she soon picked up the gist of what they were doing and could easily have done a good bit better, given half a chance.

'If I can get my laptop all sorted, rigged up and running again I should be able to make some headway in a better direction and then we shall be able to buy more nice things to eat,' Bardwell went on optimistically.

Bardwell was already beginning to feel a good bit more cheerful, for he had noticed that his old work ethic was slowly coming back again after a rather depressing lull.

'I think it is a good idea to go about things together rather than on our own,' said Rilganna to Bardwell. 'I have found this whole experience unsettling and puzzling, and it is not over yet, as challenging things keep happening by the day.'

'I wholeheartedly agree,' replied Bardwell. He was a sensible, badger-of-the-world type of individual, but his confidence had taken quite a knock lately, what with one thing and another, and he was relieved to have Rilganna's common-sense approach, although he forgot to say so.

When they arrived back at the garden house and unlocked the oak door, they stared at each other in astonishment, for they discovered that while they had been out the ground floor had been furnished. There were now two massive armchairs and a couch, each complete with soft sky-blue cushions; the furniture was standing on planed wooden floorboards and there were small multi-coloured mats randomly scattered around. The overall effect was colourful and welcoming.

Sturdy cupboards had appeared in the kitchen, full of all the cooking utensils that Rilganna and Bardwell could only have dreamed about. There had been no need for Bardwell to have spent his money on provisions, as the new larder was full to brimming with everything they liked to eat. Bardwell felt stunned by this new development. He took off his cap and sat down, knowing now that Rilganna had been accurate in her recollection about the transformation and strange goings-on that had occurred the night before.

They had temporarily forgotten about Zig-Zag Pontoon who, having been completely charged up in their absence, was now sitting nonchalantly in the corner where they had left him.

'Did you see any of these changes happening, Zig-Zag?' asked Rilganna, who got very little back by way of a sensible reply from the dreamy robot, who continued sitting very near to the power socket, hoping with all his heart that no one was about to put him back outside.

'Well, this is a carry-on,' said Bardwell, in a kind of surprised whisper. 'I'm beginning to feel a little giddy; perhaps this is some kind of weird dream.'

Bardwell sat down on the couch and pinched his leg sharply but nothing he could see around him changed at all.

'Let's climb up the new spiral staircase that appeared the night before you arrived,' said Rilganna to Bardwell, keen to investigate and feeling braver now she had a companion, and so together they cautiously explored the upper rooms, having stumbled up the narrow stairway.

'Look at these beds; I have never seen such fine ones before,' said Bardwell, examining them closely and judging them to be stoutly manufactured of the best hardwearing materials. He investigated the newly fitted clothes cupboards and quickly came to the same conclusion.

'This bed linen is up-market and luxurious,' exclaimed Rilganna, 'and look, the duvet covers and pillowcases all have the same blue flower pattern on them.' Rilganna was beginning to find the whole experience unworldly.

Once they were over the initial shock, she and Bardwell raised their paws in joy and banged them together. The fully charged Zig-Zag Pontoon, who had followed them up the stairs, immediately struggled up onto one of the beds: he was tired, and concerned about his situation, so he just lay there staring straight ahead, legs and arms akimbo, making no conversation at all.

Meanwhile, Rilganna and Bardwell slowly ventured back downstairs again and hesitatingly switched on the central heating system which had been installed in their absence; they listened with pleasure as the boiler burst into life and started to hum happily with a reassuring rhythm.

'Is the small robot a friend of yours, Rilganna?' asked Bardwell, feeling that he had to make some kind of comment about the metal occupant.

'No, I have only recently met him. He banged on the door early the other morning, having run out of energy. He was completely exhausted, and I managed to drag him inside to plug his lead into the wall socket. I don't have the heart to turn him out again; I couldn't do that as he has nowhere else to go,' said Rilganna, in a definite tone which made it quite clear that Zig-Zag was there to stay.

'Will you be staying here too, Bardwell?' Rilganna asked. She could hardly bear to imagine how she would feel if Bardwell had said no.

'Yes, I'd like to stick around, if that's okay,' Bardwell replied, and nothing further needed to be said as they were both completely content with the situation.

'I think the best thing to do is to bring Zig-Zag Pontoon back downstairs and make a comfortable bed for him near to the power socket, so that if he has a funny turn, he can plug himself in again without difficulty,' said Rilganna, being practical.

This arrangement went smoothly, and in fact, Zig-Zag was able to make his own way back down the stairs as he had already climbed up them in the first place, and he was more than content with Rilganna and Bardwell's plan for him.

After such an eventful and mind-blowing day they both felt tired and so, having eaten an early supper, using some of the provisions that had appeared in the larder, Rilganna and Bardwell went back upstairs, snuggled into the blissfully warm duvets that were waiting for them, turned out the lamps, and quickly fell into a deep, peaceful sleep.

The next few days went pleasantly by and a kind of unplanned daily way of doing things was emerging between them.

Zig-Zag Pontoon said very little and did even less, but he kept himself fully charged up and seemed to be happy enough zigging around as the mood took him. After all, anything was better than that awful factory. He was still having nasty imaginings about being wrapped in that bubble pack stuff ready to be sealed up in a box for despatch. He was hoping to stay forever in the garden house with the other two and as Rilganna and Bardwell hadn't mentioned anything about his having to leave he was beginning to feel more contented and settled by the day.

3

Peckleton

One night during the following week there was a violent winter storm: hailstones almost as big as gobstoppers pelted down from the heavens, banging against the windows of the garden house, and bouncing ferociously onto the ground beneath. The trees moaned and groaned under the pressure of wind, rain and hail, and twigs were being thrown here, there and everywhere. Rilganna and Bardwell woke up at the same time to the noise of the storm and to an odd scratching sound coming from outside. Bardwell felt he should deal with the situation, being a good bit sturdier than Rilganna, although he was a little fearful about what he might find as he himself was not particularly substantial in stature and a persistent intruder might be difficult to see off. He switched on the torch, which was resting on the windowsill, drew himself up to his full height and peered out.

At first he could see nothing in the darkness of the stormy night, and then he caught sight of a black spaniel dog, noticeable in the gloom by his light-coloured cap. He had no overcoat on and was completely drenched. His trainers were waterlogged, and his cap was so sopping wet that it was hardly distinguishable from an old rag. The spaniel whined and shook pitifully as he did his best to avoid the descending avalanche of freezing gobstoppers from the skies. Bardwell looked towards Rilganna, who shook her head in agreement, and so together they went down the spiral staircase and unlocked the oak door.

'Oh dear, I'm really sorry to wake you so late on in the night,' said the shivering spaniel apologetically, clutching at the dripping cap he had removed from his head and feeling more than surprised that anyone had heard him above the noise of the horrific storm, 'but I'm in such a bad way. May I sleep on your floor overnight to dry out? Then I shall be off out of your way early in the morning.'

The black spaniel, who had soft floppy eye-catching ears, ended the sentence with an enormous sneeze, while at the same time trying to squeeze the rainwater out of his sodden and bedraggled cap.

'Indeed, you can rest up here for the night,' said Bardwell. 'Come on in out of this terrible weather and get warm.'

'My name is Peckleton,' said the spaniel, first shaking Bardwell's paw and then Rilganna's. 'I know it's not a cool-sounding name but it's the only one I've ever had.'

'I would consider Peckleton to be a trendy enough name,' said Bardwell, 'and I bet Rilganna will think the same.'

Rilganna straightaway confirmed that Peckleton's name was as hip as any other name she had ever heard spoken, so the matter was quickly settled.

With introductions all done and sorted, and having removed his wet trainers, Peckleton dried down his wet coat with a towel that Rilganna took from the warm radiator, and gradually he began to perk up. Bardwell soon tipped out the excess water from Peckleton's trainers and put his cap on the radiator to dry off a bit. Rilganna wouldn't hear of Peckleton sleeping on the floor, as he was still shivering and his fur still looked a bit damp, so after a warm mug of hot milky chocolate and a crumbly shortbread biscuit Rilganna made a cosy bed for him upstairs, where the exhausted visitor was relieved to snuggle down for the night. Before long the contented sound of protracted snores and sniffs was heard throughout the upper floor of the convivial household.

In the morning Rilganna was downstairs first as she was accustomed to an early start and preferred it that way. Once Bardwell and Peckleton were awake, and with their morning showers put to one side, they all sat together at the large wooden table in the kitchen. As they enjoyed large beakers of tea and ate their creamy porridge and toast, they were smiling, chatting a lot and recalling the terrible downpour from the night before.

'I don't wish to pry,' said diplomatic Bardwell to Peckleton, having changed the subject from the inclement weather, and feeling curious as to why a small dog should have been out in such an horrific storm, 'but I was wondering how you got into such a sorry situation, as to be honest, Peckleton, you looked pretty off the boil last night.'

Peckleton rested against the back of the chair and then put his head down onto his front paws. He didn't want to talk about himself at first, as he felt self-conscious, but Rilganna gently tapped the top of his head by way of encouragement and gradually he started to tell his story.

'I got involved with some bad company,' said Peckleton, mumbling a little. 'I was drifting down a path leading towards big trouble. I knew it was a mistake to have got tied up with such a nasty lot. Locally they were known as the Spherical Horde and the very utterance of their name caused shudders in the heart of many. It all seemed exciting at first but once I was initiated into the gang I was trapped. The other night, while the gang members were fast asleep, I felt a strong urge to escape before I got too deeply involved in things that I didn't want to do. It was an intense sensation, just as though something, although I can't say exactly what, had taken over my mind and was instructing me to move on that very minute: it was a kind of detached thought process over which I had no influence. I hope this makes sense,' said Peckleton, trying to clarify what had happened to him and finding it hard to come up with the right words.

'Yes, it makes sense,' said Bardwell. Although they had never experienced such a thing themselves, he and Rilganna instinctively understood what Peckleton was trying to describe and sympathised with him, as he tried to explain something that was not quite tangible in the normal way of things.

They continued looking intently at the new arrival as he carried on with his intriguing tale.

'There was enough money in my pocket for a fare and so I crept silently out of the house and ran and ran as fast as my legs would carry me. I saw a coach waiting in the coach station, with Landsmoth written on the front, and so I jumped onto it, although I didn't know where I was going as I hadn't heard of Landsmoth before. My fare wouldn't take me all the way to the coach's final destination, and so I had to get off at this small village of Crindling when my ticket ran out. Walking along in the pouring rain and hail, I saw your garden house with its outside lamp glowing and feelings of hope filled my heart. I was wondering whether I could chance rattling at the door to see if anyone was about when you came downstairs to see what was going on.'

'Well, we are very glad to see you, aren't we, Rilganna?'

Rilganna once more confirmed Bardwell's statement to be completely true.

At this point Peckleton, having eaten his breakfast and finished his second beaker of hot milky tea, got up from the chair, stretched his legs and put on his trainers, still wet from the downpour, and tried to straighten out his equally damp cap.

He thanked Rilganna and Bardwell with all his heart for their kindness and, having waved a paw at Zig-Zag Pontoon, who was staring at him quizzically, he made his way towards the door.

The two looked anxiously at each other and with a nod of confirmation from Rilganna, Bardwell said, 'Look, Peckleton, we have both been down on our luck big time, and you have too, and goodness only knows what story Zig-Zag Pontoon has to tell, as we have yet to hear the details. To be honest we don't know where we are either, or what the future holds. It seems to us that we all have much in common, so how about your staying here until you are sorted and if you want to move on and find your fortune elsewhere after a few weeks, of course you would be free to do so with no harm done.'

Peckleton, who could hardly believe what he had just

heard, started to make a monotonous humming noise which in turn led to a high-pitched whine brought on by relief at his good fortune. Rilganna thought it best to get Peckleton quickly involved in something completely different to take his mind off the situation, and so without further ado that is how it all got sorted. Bardwell and the newcomer climbed up the spiral stairway together, like the firm friends they now were, and tidied up all three duvets ready for them to use that night, and left Rilganna pondering about what could possibly happen next.

4

Daxham Arrives

All things considered, Rilganna, Bardwell, Peckleton and Zig-Zag Pontoon settled down well together, and the next couple of months went scurrying by. Sometimes, when they returned from one of their outings, they found that more changes had happened in or around the garden house, and although they were always excited by any new developments that occurred, they were no longer as puzzled and thrown over as they once were.

There were clothes in the upstairs cupboards suitable for the three who needed them (Zig-Zag excepted); one day a tall perimeter fence appeared down each side of the garden area; and shortly afterwards they noticed that a carved wooden house name had become attached to the brickwork by the side of the oak front door, and so Waters-edge was now the much-loved home of Rilganna, Bardwell, Peckleton and Zig-Zag Pontoon.

Each new day was brimming with activities for the residents of Waters-edge. They were happy together, never bored, and felt disappointed when darkness fell, and it was time for them to have their evening drink and close down their undertakings until the next day.

Mesmerised by their tranquil surroundings, they could often be seen gazing into the river at the bottom of the garden with its soft curving bank and backdrop of oak, silver birch and willow trees, with multifarious bushes growing in between. The water was free-flowing and sparkling with clumps of yellow-flowering water irises and marsh marigolds growing in abundance along its perimeter. Wads of watercress flourished thickly in beds, and little silvery fish hurried here and there, going about their daily business. As the sun peeped through the gaps in the branches of the trees, heavily laden with the bright green leaves of spring and summer, the resulting glints of shimmering light generated ever-changing reflections on the surface of the water. Bardwell, Rilganna, Peckleton and Zig-Zag were enchanted by their environment, whatever the weather.

Hibberley Heron was a frequent visitor to the riverbank and would often stop on by to pass the time of day, but he never had the time to chat for long. He was always impatient to get going again. His window cleaning business had been growing steadily for some time and with so many demanding clients to satisfy he was in a rush all day long. He hardly had enough time to eat his packed lunch, which he prepared each morning. In fact, he was beginning to look rather peaky and overworked.

Peckleton became responsible for all the exterior projects at Waters-edge because of his love of outdoor pursuits. Zig-

Zag Pontoon helped Peckleton as the small robot was able to zip through any gardening and do-it-yourself jobs without a second's thought; that was what he had been programmed to do at the factory and he was still very keen to keep up his skill base. In spite of all this activity, Zig-Zag had plenty of spare time left to keep polished up, and as a consequence he always looked well turned-out. He regularly made sure that his workings were fully charged up just in case of an unexpected power outage and in an abstract kind of way the others had become fond of him.

Rilganna and Bardwell had recently designed and manufactured a kind of gardening-cum-working-dog's apron for Peckleton. It was a stout woven linen apron with numerous pockets of differing sizes and depths sewn into the front and sides of the garment, including a small pocket near the top of the apron which was complete with a zip fastener where Peckleton could keep his shed keys. He had a habit of losing them, as they would often tumble out from the pocket of his old gardening pull-ups as he bent around; eventually he would find them hidden somewhere in a flower bed after frantic searching and much exasperation. In the larger pockets of his new apron, he was able to keep his gardening implements or his everyday tools if he was undertaking repairs.

Bardwell, with his laptop now set up to his satisfaction, spent many a long hour encouraging his small fiscal resource to grow as he carefully studied the financial marketplace. If there was any money left over after their expenses were paid Bardwell would put it to one side for their future use, particularly in readiness for any unexpected emergencies. Bardwell was a wise and clever badger who was determined that no one at Waters-edge would find themselves with an overdrawn balance while he was able to network away at his laptop. His recent experience of homelessness and finding that he was unable to make ends meet had left Bardwell feeling insecure, and he was now a very cautious and wary badger: any recklessness that he once embraced in his former life had completely vanished from his thought process.

While out for a walk one day, Bardwell came across Mr Yaxlie Owl, a well-established accountant-cum-financial-advisor who had an impressive tree house office situated in a huge sycamore tree on the opposite riverbank. His headquarters, as he called his workplace, had a swish reception area which was softly lit by cleverly concealed lighting. The melodic sound of song thrush and blackbird, gathered together in choirs and synchronising delightfully together, issued out from a discreet CD player positioned near the ultra-modern ultra-precise hot drinks machine: there was no risk of coffee unexpectedly percolating out from this machine when the hot chocolate button had been selected, although the newfangled device was known to overheat from time to time, filling the area with steam.

The walls of the reception area were well-painted in a relaxing light green and tall leafy plants in large containers were positioned in all four corners of the open-plan area. A plush wall-to-wall light beige carpet covered the floor; there were four bright red bucket-style chairs strategically positioned near to wooden bookcases full of books, and the latest bird and wildlife magazines were available for clients to look through while they awaited attention. Yaxlie boasted state-of-the-art electronic aids in his office and all financial dealings were carried out with great expediency. Yaxlie had a successful business and was rather pleased with how life in general had turned out for him.

As their acquaintance developed, Yaxlie became impressed by Bardwell's understanding of the financial landscape and an arrangement developed between them whereby Yaxlie paid Bardwell a modest payment in exchange for the market research he did on his behalf, an arrangement which suited them both.

Farallina Fox was Yaxlie Owl's receptionist and personal assistant, and he relied on her help in the office. She lived in Foxglove Cottage, which had a tiny back garden, but she had a substantial allotment not far from her home where she could dig, root out and grow all kinds of vegetables and flowers in her spare time. During the summer months the front garden at Foxglove Cottage had a beautiful display of dusky pink roses where fragrant blooms the size of saucepan lids filled the air with a beguiling heady perfume, which attracted passers-by who stopped in their stride to sniff in the sweet-scented air.

One particular morning Peckleton had been out for his usual early morning jog along the lanes, having been settling in new trainers he had recently bought. As it was a lovely spring day and being satisfied that there was no indication of early morning frosts on the horizon, he decided to get busy in the garden, planting out French beans, lettuces, radishes and other tasty eatables; he had created a kitchen garden for Rilganna and Bardwell, who both loved cooking and making soup. Rilganna's favourite treat was a freshly picked mixed green salad which she liked to eat with some local cheddar cheese tucked into a sandwich, using their home-baked bread. Farallina, who was Peckleton's best friend, often called on by at Waters-edge when he was working in the garden and they regularly swapped plants, cuttings, and horticultural tips about vegetables, salad leaves and soft fruits.

On this particular morning Peckleton was so engrossed in his market gardening that he hadn't noticed the arrival of a tatty old boat at the river's edge. Suddenly the peaceful and harmonious environment was shattered and Peckleton heard a great kerfuffle, an almighty splash and a lot of noisy high-pitched squeaking. Peckleton put down his gardening tools and hurried down to the riverbank. To his astonishment he saw a substantially sized penguin with a lifebelt firmly secured round his middle. The penguin was wearing a yellow and blue striped nautical style suit which was far too tight, and he was shouting, 'Help – penguin overboard!' It seemed that the boatman had been climbing out of his craft, had missed his flipper hold and fallen into the water. Peckleton had never come across a penguin with a lifebelt on before and could hardly believe what he was seeing.

'Save me!' shouted the sailor in sheer desperation, and at the top of his voice.

'Swim,' shouted Peckleton in reply. 'You are a penguin, for goodness sake, swim.'

With a great deal of splashing, struggle and panic the plump penguin finally managed to manoeuvre himself into the side of the river and eventually climbed onto the bank; completely shocked and disorientated, his lifebelt was still tightly attached around his middle. However, after a short pause he made a sudden recovery and with great gusto shouted out to Peckleton, 'Bring up my bags, there's a good fellow,' and then this rather presumptuous creature waddled up the garden and through the open back door into the kitchen of Waters-edge.

Rilganna was taken aback to see the sudden appearance of a stranger. The penguin was creating puddles on the kitchen floor, and she was dumbfounded by his rudeness. She shouted to Bardwell, who quickly hurried down the spiral stairway to see what was going on.

Meanwhile, Peckleton, with great difficulty, had managed to pull the penguin's old boat up out of the water and onto the riverbank and, yes, amazingly, was carrying his two bulky bags up to the back door of Waters-edge.

A mug of elderberry juice and a slice of fruit cake, reluctantly offered by Rilganna to the fractious visitor, quickly comforted him in his soaking plight, so much so that he looked around the room and with some conviction commented, 'I must say this place is very cosy; it would suit me very nicely.'

It was an extraordinary sight to see a bedraggled penguin firmly attached to a lifebelt becoming more disagreeable with every word he spoke. In just a few minutes the interloper had started to act as though he was about to take up residence at Waters-edge.

'Who are you?' asked Rilganna, becoming rather irritated, and then without waiting for a reply, she said, 'I'm afraid we don't take in lodgers or paying guests here but in the next lane there is a bed and breakfast establishment that takes in "respectable" tourists.'

On hearing this the penguin began quivering in a rather strange way: he started to make a loud groaning noise, complaining of pains all over his body, exclaiming that he had probably picked up a deadly virus from that "dirty river water".

'I think the penguin is suffering from exhaustion,' said Bardwell, trying a non-confrontational approach. 'Perhaps he should rest up here for a while, as he has had a rather nasty shock, and after a good night's sleep he can go on his way tomorrow as obviously he must have his plans.'

Come the next morning, the penguin was up and doing as dawn broke and by the time Rilganna had arrived downstairs, he was already sitting comfortably in an armchair with his slippers on, reading a tatty old paperback book and looking very much at home.

'My name is Daxham,' said the uninvited guest, and repeating what he had said the previous day confirmed that the little house would suit him very nicely.

'You are astonishingly discourteous and inconsiderate,' said Rilganna bluntly. 'Why have you come here anyway? No one has invited you.' Not unexpectedly Rilganna received no reply.

However many times Rilganna quizzed Daxham, she couldn't quite fathom him out, or pin down anything he said that remotely hinted at truthfulness. In fact, this unwanted arrival was more like a tricky slippery eel, and quite unlike the usual type of visitor that anyone might normally expect (or want) to meet. What's more, he appeared to have no recollection of where he used to live or where he was actually going.

Realising that an awkward situation was developing, and after yet another protracted pause, Daxham suddenly said, 'The fact of the matter is that on the spur of the moment I decided to go cruising on my boat. I started my purposeful journey from further downstream and, as I experienced the wind propelling me along, I felt as free as a bird in the sky.

Having thought reflectively during my meditative journey there became no doubt in my mind that the right time in life had arrived for me to make my fortune, when of course the right outlet had materialised for one or more of my many exceptional talents, yet to be exploited. Unfortunately, as it turned out, I lost my bearings during my meanderings and went completely off course.'

The whole explanation was very odd. Daxham certainly didn't give the impression that he was multi-gifted, in fact quite the opposite. The only statement he made that seemed to be at all plausible was that he had got lost, although it was not really clear where he was actually aiming to go.

The residents of Waters-edge concluded that the mysterious caller was in a state of disarray and completely out of kilter with reality. If he was trying to endear himself to his new acquaintances, he was certainly going the wrong way about it.

Having thought about the situation, Bardwell whispered a suggestion to Peckleton.

'Perhaps it would be a good idea to tidy up Daxham's boat, Peckleton, if you think you can manage it, place it back in the river with his luggage safely inside, and then we can escort the penguin down to the riverbank for his departure?'

Peckleton went straight off. He was pleased that Bardwell had made this suggestion, as he felt he had already wasted enough time on this unwelcome stranger and wanted to get back to his market gardening.

When the boat and the sailor were prepared for a fresh launch, Rilganna, Peckleton, Bardwell and Zig-Zag Pontoon stood at the riverbank, ready to wave the penguin off in good time, before there was any chance of the light dwindling, as the weather had turned out rather murky.

To their horror, as Daxham climbed into the boat his body began to shake and quiver, and his flippers flapped so violently that he overturned the small vessel, and the unfortunate Peckleton felt obliged to jump in and assist the penguin, who seemed unable or unwilling to swim; he was in a state of the most terrible panic and alarm and his flippers were flying everywhere.

'Please, please can I stay here with you?' Daxham blurted out anxiously, when he was on dry land and had recovered a little from his ordeal. 'I can undertake river tours with my boat to earn my keep; none of you will regret it for one minute, I can promise that. I am a penguin with a great deal of ambition. Can't you see it bursting out through my beak and travelling down to the tips of my side feathers?'

These outrageous and bizarre claims were quite ridiculous. Daxham seemed unable to swim properly or, if he could, he certainly didn't like getting wet. He was unstable in his boat, which was in a poor state of repair and fit only for the scrap yard, so how he thought he was going to undertake tours that anyone would want to risk life, limb or feather for was a mystery to them all.

To this very day there is still uncertainty as to how this came about but the boat got tied up again, the soaking wet luggage came back into Waters-edge and Daxham settled down to live with them. At times the penguin's behaviour was almost too trying for words, but as the weeks went on, no one at Waters-edge would have wanted to lose him as he was so full of life and irrational optimism. The downside was that his tricky and unpredictable way of carrying on continued, much as it had started, with little likelihood of improvement.

5

An Unexpected Magical Phenomenon

Bardwell was feeling a little light-headed one morning and so he sat down on the round wicker chair by the window overlooking the garden. He casually picked up a small book that had been lying on the window ledge for some time and which no one had taken any notice of (in fact Bardwell thought he felt the book nudge his paw, although looking back he could not be "absolutely" sure that he had not imagined this).

Anyway, he nonchalantly sat glancing through the pages and then began reading some of the poems and riddles that the book contained. It was an odd little publication illustrated with brightly coloured pictures that seemed to bear no resemblance to what was on the rest of the page. As he got to the end of the book, he noticed that something weird was happening; random words were appearing on what had previously been a blank cover sheet. As sentences developed from the muddle of words they began to pulsate until they became a readable message which was a little confusing, while at the same time revealing information that acquainted Bardwell with an *Understanding* relating to an astonishing fact.

> *The following is the key to open up the chance for temporary withdrawal from the normal range of vision. Please note that these Instructions only become evident to those considered suitable to receive this unique gift, so for those found to be eligible it will be possible for invisibility to be granted at the drop of a brass button!*

Bardwell strained his eyes and concentrated on reading the additional text that was coming next. It went on to explain how the gift might be activated.

> *The gifted contender must deeply meditate on the vision of a pond full of water lilies and goldfish, situated in a large field of daffodils, while at the same time gently rubbing his or her head.*

Bardwell, being a curious type of badger, couldn't resist testing this conundrum and so, having followed the rather obscure *Instructions,* he glanced into the long mirror and found that his image was in fact gradually fading, and he watched until it had completely vanished. Panicking a little, as he had absolutely no desire to remain invisible, he shook his head three times and then rubbed his forehead hard, this being the guidance for disabling the conundrum that had also appeared on the empty page.

Bardwell soon found that his visible being was slowly re-emerging, which was an enormous relief as he was beginning to feel rather insecure and had no desire to disappear.

That evening, after their meal was over, Bardwell asked if anyone had ever looked through the little book on the windowsill and whether they had noticed anything unusual as a result. Rilganna, Peckleton and Daxham, looking puzzled, went to investigate the book of poems and riddles. One after another they waited patiently to see whether the information and *Instructions* that Bardwell had read on the back page would come again, and to their astonishment the unique *Understanding* reappeared to all three of them in turn.

Like Bardwell, they had all been granted the gift of temporary invisibility to be used at will, along with the capability to re-emerge again. It was not unsurprising that they were made a little anxious by this mystery, but they had already had plenty of practice at coping with bizarre goings-on and this was just another phase of discovery that they needed to take on board and deal with.

Zig-Zag was not at all interested in this novelty and certainly didn't want to join in with the others. The small robot had enough to think about, ensuring that his workings were always topped up with energy via the power point, and had no wish to complicate his situation further and risk any unexpected complications by fading away, even if it was just a temporary arrangement.

Bardwell remained restless for most of the night, thinking about this new revelation. Discovering that they all shared this rare and precious gift was, in his opinion, an additional burden that they could have done without. He found himself biting his paw, which was a habit he had developed when he became nervous; he tried very hard to break the inclination but found it impossible to resist when his worries became out of control. Now he wished that he had never opened the wretched book.

The next morning, while they sat eating their breakfast together, Bardwell said, 'I hope you all agree that what we discovered yesterday was a great privilege but also a responsibility that we could have done without. I think we should be undeterred by the revelation and keep it a safe secret between ourselves forever.'

'I was thinking the same thing,' said Rilganna. 'In fact, I have been thinking about it all night. Let's stand up and make this pledge here and now.'

One after another they all said, 'Pledge made and agreed.'

Daxham kept his promise to keep the secret and surprisingly never once let them down, irresponsible though he so often was.

They carried on with their lives, having decided to put this unexpected newly discovered magical mystery out of their minds. Nevertheless, Bardwell could not help wondering whether one day it might come in useful, although for the moment he could not imagine what they would need it for!

6

Deptus Dickens, Burgatus Bulldog and Belltring Bulldog

Deptus Dickens, a magnificent black cat with thick shiny fur and long delicate whiskers, presented himself to the world with considerable impression. He lived in an elegant penthouse suite on the top of the highest of high-rise apartment blocks called Fremont House. This prestigious building was situated in the midst of a fashionable area called Enterprise Wharf, which was widely recognised as the natural home of the successful and up-and-coming. It was situated in close proximity to the widest reaches of the River Rushmore, in the capital city of Glenland, which was called Dunlace.

This residential tower with its flamboyant appearance was renowned as a modern masterpiece, having been designed by one of the most gifted and distinguished contemporary architects in the kingdom of Glenland, namely one Sir Archibald Sprigot. It was constructed with stout steel girders and finished in glittering translucent glass, curvaceously shaped and moulded to perfection. Well-tended gardens encircled the perimeter of the building, and it was obvious that supervision of the green area was undertaken by an enthusiastic gardener or gardeners of impressive ability.

Late in the evening, after a long day of activity, Deptus would sit in his spacious sitting room with its full-height windows, watching the lights of the pleasure cruisers flickering and dancing on the surface of the River Rushmore as they gently meandered along. Neatly zipped up in his comfortable leisure suit and wearing his softly moulded indoor trainers, he imbibed this iconic view with great pleasure as he enjoyed his evening meal, his dish perched on a small wooden table. By and large Deptus was a most contented cat.

Fremont House was not far from a peaceful riverside walk and park which was full of trees, bushes and tidily kept flower beds. Numerous comfortable teak benches of pleasing design were readily available for those wishing to recline awhile to take in the air. Deptus was the kind of cat who, if he was feeling the need for a little contemplation as dusk was approaching, would enjoy a slow stroll around the park's perimeter. As you probably know, twilight is the time of day when cats do most of their thinking.

It was hard to define exactly how Deptus had made his fortune. Those envious of his success had a tendency to describe him as a wheeler and dealer. Sometimes this term is used unfairly to describe someone like Deptus when a more accurate and appropriate description does not immediately come to mind, but in his case any negative or derogatory implication often attached to this label was completely without foundation. Deptus was without a doubt a skilled broker of deals with a sound reputation, and a more respected and decent cat was hard to find anywhere in the city of Dunlace or indeed beyond. It was widely known within the commercial and banking fraternity that Deptus' word and firm paw shake was as solid as a gold-plated fishbowl.

Deptus had been orphaned, so had learnt to fend for himself. He understood that he needed to follow his natural survival instincts if he was not to end up in a bad situation. He trained himself to be quick-thinking and far-sighted and soon realised that he had a natural gift for sensing the worth of any potential prospect that showed up on his horizon.

As already explained, Fremont House was an exclusive high-rise apartment block and it was not easy to gain entry. Any stranger trying this was met with robust interrogation. There was a security swipe-card arrangement in operation at the main door of the apartment block, and at the reception desk there sat the ever-vigilant Burgatus Bulldog.

Burgatus Bulldog lived with Belltring Bulldog in their apartment at Fremont House. Belltring had an unadventurous code of dress (some might say a little on the frumpy side), but she was always cleanly and trimly turned out; no jeans with splits in the knees for her. She had a lively personality but in tandem with this she was very protective of Burgatus and became tetchy if he was disadvantaged by others' thoughtlessness. She was straight-talking and meticulous in all her doings; it was a bad idea to go against her unless there was good reason!

Deptus and Burgatus Bulldog's friendship went back a

long way and when the last incumbent of the receptionist-cum-caretaker post had been persuaded to leave on account of a suspicious irregularity in the stamp and petty cash box, Deptus straightaway thought of Burgatus as a possible replacement. He had recently resigned from his job in the fish market, due to increasing discomfort from his arthritis which badly affected his wellbeing, particularly during inclement weather – a state of affairs made worse by the handling of cold, damp fish.

Fremont House was a cat-only establishment and when Deptus put Burgatus' name forward at the annual meeting of the Residents Association as an ideal applicant to fill the vacant position of receptionist-cum-caretaker there was some hesitation and whispers of dissent, as you might imagine.

It fell to Burgatus Bulldog to give a persuasive talk to the assembled gathering of the Association about his credentials for carrying out the job in a professional and fair-minded way, and to explain about his high standards while taking care not to sound too cantankerous, which was a tricky balance. With his excellent references from the fish market, where in fact most of the cats now recognised him from, and with the congenial and kindly Belltring Bulldog right by his side, most residents were pleased to endorse his appointment, with a few reservations, although they all managed an enthusiastic clap when a vote was taken and found to be overwhelmingly positive in his favour. The decision was therefore declared done and dusted by Deptus Dickens, acting in his capacity as chairman of the Residents Association.

It was fortuitous, and an unexpected surprise for Burgatus, that with the receptionist-cum-caretaker post there came, as part of a generous employment package, a rent-free apartment and a couple of other benefits like refreshments while on duty. Belltring was over the moon with the news when Burgatus was appointed to his new job and they were able to move into the new accommodation at Fremont House, as the living quarters near the fish market were not at all to her liking, mainly because of the lingering fishy odour which permeated their small home, particularly in the hot summer months when the windows were open, and she was more than pleased to vacate the rooms. She was in fact so glad to escape that she left all their old furniture and belongings behind, much to Burgatus' chagrin, although he soon got over his discontentment as he was incapable of being out of humour with Belltring for more than three minutes at any one time.

Inspired by a sitting room blessed with the gift of natural light and sun, Belltring spent most of Burgatus' pay-out from his previous job, which he received on account of the loyal and dedicated service he had given at the fish market, on hard and soft furnishings, pictures and other tasteful embellishments obtained after successful bidding at the auction rooms, where she combined her artistic talents with her bargaining abilities. Burgatus was very appreciative of Belltring's proficient negotiating skills, and as she was renowned for spotting things of worth in the sale rooms and obtaining them at knock-down prices, there was harmony between them.

The only item about which they quarrelled was a cuckoo clock made of dreary dark wood. In spite of Burgatus putting it out at the side of the recycling bin each week when the collection was due, it always reappeared back on the kitchen wall the following morning, where it continued to make irritating calls at random times, often competing with Burgatus' loud bouts of snoring and snorting during the night-time hours; this did not trouble him, of course, as he was out for the count.

Soon their apartment was a home that they both enjoyed spending time in. Having a state-of-the-art spacious curved balcony with stunning views across the River Rushmore, Belltring found inspiration in seeking out attractively shaped flowerpots, which she filled with sweet-smelling plants. She found some striking garden ornaments at the auction rooms which fitted in very well with their new environment and soon there were two reclining sun-loungers with accompanying umbrellas and a picnic table with matching chairs; all of which were established in the sunny corners of their treasured outside space.

The balconies at Fremont House were all fitted with white awnings that could be electronically activated to pull down and open up at the touch of a button to protect the outdoor areas from strong sunlight, so that even on the hottest of hot summer days the two devoted Bulldogs were as blissfully comfortable as two could possibly be reclining on their comfortable balcony chairs listening to their favourite ballet music, eating crisps and watching the river craft, large and small, pass across their eyeline.

Deptus and the Bulldogs' taste in music was completely at odds; Deptus preferred to get lost in the strong rhythmic beat of the latest pop scene which excited his imagination and stirred his paws; the louder the volume the more he enjoyed it.

Burgatus declared that he planned to spend the rest of his working life doing this terrific new job. He did not mind how many hours he spent at the reception area or on any of the other responsibilities that went with the post; in fact, apart from his everyday life with Belltring, it became a mainstay of his life, and he was never seemingly "off-duty".

There had been bouts of disruption in the past with dubious undesirables hanging about outside the main door of the apartment block, waiting for an opportunity to get inside to make mischief, but Burgatus, although he often looked as though he was napping, was as bright as a button and twice as quick. In one of his previous deployments in the city's police department he had been part of the support staff attached to an important task force (the details of which he would never discuss) so with his natural instinct for spotting anything that was not quite right he was able to immediately home in on any suspicious activity, and he regularly used this well-honed ability to prevent dubious antisocial behaviour developing into a full-blown threat.

The cat-eenagers at Fremont House loved to get out and about if they had the opportunity. Having crept past their sleeping seniors, some would try to escape late at night to join revellers at the nearby Cat Club. However, they met with a sticky end, as they never quite made it to the main door before they were picked up in a most unflattering manner and escorted back to their respective apartments by Burgatus, who considered the Cat Club to be a most disreputable venue and completely off-limits. Most only tried it the once, especially when the new CCTV system was installed and there was little or no chance of sneaking past the reception area.

Toddy and Tilly lived in adjoining apartments with their families and were great friends, but Toddy was a full-on socially inclined hip cat who liked to take advantage of the nightlife that the locality had on offer, if he had only half a chance of getting out of Fremont House and back again before anyone noticed he was missing. He persuaded Tilly to join him for the much-advertised all-night rave at the Cat Club. Toddy took some money from the pocket of his senior's trousers, which were hanging on a convenient peg, and crept out of the apartment where he met Tilly on the landing as arranged. Tilly was reluctant because she knew that she would be in trouble if she was caught going out without her seniors' say-so, and she was also dubious about trying to sneak past Burgatus Bulldog unnoticed.

'I am worried,' said little Tilly. 'I have heard that Burgatus Bulldog thinks that the Cat Club should be shut down and shuttered up, and I have also heard that he can get fierce when he gets cross, and what if he catches us; what shall we do then?'

'Oh, don't worry about that dopey Burgatus Bulldog,' said Toddy to Tilly, who was already looking rather pasty and not at all sure that she wanted to go out at all. 'He's always half asleep and he's three times as stupid.'

Tilly was not at all convinced, and remained hesitant, but she went along with Toddy as that was the arrangement they had made and she didn't like to go back on it.

They crept all the way down the several flights of stairs and found that Burgatus Bulldog was sitting in the reception area as usual in his comfortable night chair with his blue and red striped slippers on and a thick woollen blanket draped across his knees. He looked very much asleep, as his eyes were tightly shut, but Burgatus was never asleep on duty. He let Toddy and Tilly get almost to the main door before he suddenly got up and stooped over them just as they were about to abscond.

'And where do you think you two are going so late at night?' said Burgatus in an abrupt voice.

Toddy and Tilly froze where they stood, too shocked to make any kind of reply to Mr Bulldog's enquiry, but he knew instinctively that they were on their way out to join the all-night rave at the Cat Club as that was just the kind of activity that would catch Toddy's eye. Burgatus had been on "red alert", so to speak, all evening, anticipating Toddy's exit.

Burgatus speedily secured Toddy and temporarily put him in the stationery cupboard for safe keeping, as he had a tendency to vanish, while he returned Tilly to her apartment: he hovered outside until he was sure that she was safely inside, and the door was firmly locked behind her. He knew that it would not have been her idea for them to tip-paw off together to such a sleazy venue, and he felt sure that she would never agree to do anything like that again. Burgatus had been keeping an eye on Toddy for some weeks, as it was obvious that he was going haywire and taking little Tilly down the same path.

Toddy, on release from the stationery cupboard, pleaded with Burgatus Bulldog not to say anything to anyone about his planned night out and his recent misdemeanours, which were many.

'Please, please, Mr Bulldog, don't tell my seniors what I have been doing; they will be so angry with me. It is bad enough that those busybody teachers at the school have already complained to them about me.' Tears were welling up in Toddy's eyes and he started to tremble. Burgatus, who had a tendency to look stern, was in fact a kindly old soul and decided against any official reporting action, but he kept up his unsmiling expression while returning Toddy to his apartment as he had to be taught a lesson or two for his own wellbeing.

'Return the money to the pocket you stole it from and make yourself available at my reception desk at 6pm sharp each evening for the next week as we are going out on some walks,' said Burgatus to Toddy as he placed him on the floor by his apartment.

Toddy speedily scampered indoors and quietly shut the door behind him. He put the money back where he had got it from and silently jumped straight into his bed, feeling anxious in his mind and wishing he had never tried to go to the Cat Club's all-night rave, but it was all too late now: he stared up at his star clock on the wall and wished that he could turn back its hands.

On their evening walks together over the next week Burgatus introduced Toddy to some less fortunate cat-eenagers who lived near the park and who had messed up big time by indulging themselves in risky pastimes that had gone badly wrong for them. After these encounters, which made Toddy feel rather uncomfortable, they would circumnavigate the park, and this was when Burgatus told Toddy a few home truths.

'You don't realise how lucky you are, Toddy. You could be in the same situation as the cat-eenagers you have just met, who have no alternative but to live under the bridge near the park. They have not been spoilt and coddled along as you have been. Unfortunately, instead of being helpful and useful, you have become selfish, thoughtless, and self-indulgent. If you carry on like this, and don't take action immediately to curb your longing for the hot adventures of city life and become more settled, you will find yourself in a very nasty place. I have seen this happen before and it is not a pretty sight.'

Toddy listened, or at least pretended to, as he was bored, and as the walks and lectures were repeated for a whole week Toddy eventually took on board what Burgatus Bulldog had been saying to him and fortunately he was caught in time. He lost interest in seeking dubious nocturnal entertainment and made up his mind to try to be more resourceful, although in truth he found the idea rather uninteresting. He knew, though, that this new action would cheer others up who were embarrassed by the complaints they received with monotonous regularity about his rebellious activities, but more importantly, he was running out of plausible excuses to wriggle out of the trouble he got into!

Toddy decided that he ought to show willing and volunteer at the juniors' diving club at the swimming pool near the park on two evenings a week. His new interest enabled him to fill his spare evenings more gainfully and he behaved as though he was very enthusiastic about the club and all its activities. He was nonetheless tempted to play tricks on some of the swimmers especially if they were in earnest and a bit jittery. On one occasion he put a thick layer of margarine from a large tub he had brought from home on the edge of the diving board, but at the last minute he had to scrub it all away before the competition started as he noticed that the adjudicator was coming along to check on safety issues just before the event started, and he just about got it wiped off in time!

Belltring Bulldog was surprised and pleased to hear

about the progress that Toddy was making and although she knew he would never stay calm for long, at least for now there was a new positive spring in his step. She no longer caught Toddy messing about in the lift or jumping out from unexpected places when others were deep in thought causing shopping to be dropped, parcels to tumble down the stairs and intemperate language to explode, which happened more times than she cared to count: for now the grumbles about him had all but vanished.

Nonetheless at every turn of corner there was something novel and exciting on offer to entice Toddy away and back down the slippery path again and she feared that before long temptation would make itself known, causing his whiskers to bristle and his ears to twitch. It was hard for Toddy to be industrious when the condition called for a lot of concentration and when the regime of a constant life did not much appeal, but Burgatus had his eye on him which was not something that was easy to escape from.

Eventually Toddy saved up enough cash to invite Tilly to the Bluebell Coffee Shop for a strawberry milkshake topped with butterscotch pieces dotted with caramelised sugar, followed by three goes at the juke box: Tilly got to choose her favourite discs, so the unfortunate incident of the Cat Club rave was all but forgotten; well, if not forgotten, it was forgiven. Toddy had missed Tilly, who had ignored him for some time, and now they were together and on track again. He shared most, if not quite all, of his secrets with her and the thought of not seeing her again had made him feel miserable and insecure.

7

Albert Alsatian

It was late one evening and Deptus was on his way home from his day's work in the city. When passing Hadden Hippo's premises he heard him opening the heavy double doors of his garage-cum-workshop.

'Have you got a minute, Deptus?' said Hadden Hippo.

Deptus stepped over the road, and they went inside.

'Have you seen Albert Alsatian lately?' Hadden Hippo continued, in a troubled tone of voice.

Deptus had not chanced upon Albert for a few weeks, although he had heard that he had vacated his post as senior store detective at the department store Blisk & Blofells where he had worked for many years. Misfortune had struck him when he badly injured one of his legs during his cycling holiday in Otland last winter. He had collided with a large tree which he felt sure had moved its position just prior to his descent down a long, steep slope. After his accident, hard though he tried, he was no longer up to the demands of his energetic job and so the management transferred him to a sales vacancy in the hardware department in the basement of the store, there being no other suitable opportunities available in any of the other departments.

Albert tried to persevere, but he eventually became disheartened with his new job selling buckets, brooms and dusters. He much preferred his action-packed previous post and being cooped up all day in the basement without any natural light was the final straw, and so after one particularly bad experience, which resulted in Albert catapulting a bucket across the stockroom which hit the supervisor just as he was bending down to tie up the laces on his trainers, he decided to call it a day; on the spur of the moment he threw in his job there and then without so much as a by-your-leave.

Albert's apartment faced the back of Hadden Hippo's workshop and Hadden had noticed that just lately Albert was staring vacantly out of his window for hours on end, which was not something he normally did; he always appeared to be wearing his old red dressing gown whatever the time of day. Hadden went on to say that he would willingly find Albert a job in his workshop, but he knew that he was most impractical when it came to electro-mechanical matters.

'If you get time, Deptus, can you call on Albert out of the blue and see how things really are with him? Because if I go round to see him, he'll think I've been snooping, as his front window is clearly visible from the back of my garage workshop,' Hadden said, with concern in his voice.

Deptus agreed to do this for Hadden Hippo during the next few days and continued his journey home, but Albert's situation began to worry Deptus, and he grew as concerned about his old friend as Hadden was. He felt that he could not let matters rest and so on his way home the very next afternoon he called on him.

Albert seemed to take forever to get to his door and he was indeed wearing his dressing gown and down-at-heel slippers at 4pm. Albert didn't immediately invite Deptus into his flat and so Deptus invited himself in. He found Albert's accommodation to be in a state of disarray. His bedroom door was wide open, and from a quick perusal Deptus could tell that he had not tidied his bed for some considerable time, as a great pile of bed clothes lay haphazardly here, there and everywhere. Dirty mugs, plates and half-eaten snacks that were beginning to look musty were perched precariously on surfaces, and an old duvet was flung over his settee; things generally were not looking good.

'Are you having an early night?' asked Deptus, trying to appear casual about Albert still wearing his dressing gown so late on in the afternoon.

'It's not worth getting dressed these days, as I am going nowhere, doing nothing and seeing no one,' replied Albert, in a dull and unresponsive tone.

Although Deptus was not keen on domestic chores he insisted on tidying up Albert's bed, which didn't go down at all well with Albert, but Deptus persevered. He then rinsed up the dirty mugs and plates and put the stale old snacks in the rubbish bin.

After saying their farewells, Deptus had the impression that he had left Albert slightly more cheerful than he found him, as he had been able to impart little bits of local gossip which had given him something different to think about.

Just lately Deptus had noticed that Burgatus was spending very many hours in the reception area at Fremont House and Belltring was seeing little of him; so much so that she was making her patchwork quilts and knitted squares at a great rate of knots, with so much free time available to her each evening and at the weekends.

It was the normal routine that on Friday mornings Belltring would go shopping at the marketplace to buy all manner of tasty fresh food, and in the evening Deptus would join the Bulldogs for a delicious feast in their apartment, as his penthouse suite was in close proximity. The conversations invariably got very lively with bouts of blustery laughter filling the room. Burgatus embellished his storytelling with great panache; they had heard his tales more than once before, but as the finer points changed quite regularly, they were always fresh and entertaining.

Deptus and Burgatus had struck up a rapport as soon as they met at the fish stall in the marketplace. Once their friendship grew, they combined their knowledge and experience of life to improve their livelihoods and their trust in each other was unstinting. Burgatus knew only too well how hard Deptus had worked to keep his whiskers above water and to acquire his penthouse apartment. Burgatus was Deptus' brother-in-arms, or so he once said after he had drunk a full beaker of rum for "medicinal reasons" to stem off the onset of a chesty cold, which he was rather susceptible to, and having heard the expression on the radio the night before.

Sometimes Deptus and Burgatus would spend whole evenings together, playing dominoes in the reception area without realising how much time had slipped by, which is so often the case when the closest of friends get lost in the comfort of each other's company.

Anyway, on this particular Friday evening, Deptus told them about Albert's problems and asked Burgatus how he would feel about having a deputy to assist him with his duties so that he could have a more leisurely lifestyle. Burgatus liked the sound of this idea, and Belltring was enthusiastic too, so with this encouraging news in mind Deptus called round to see Albert again the following day. On this occasion he was pleased to see the visitor and invited Deptus into his flat.

Deptus, sitting down comfortably on Albert's large couch, came out with the following suggestion.

'I have an opportunity you might like to avail yourself of, Albert, but you will need to sharpen yourself up a bit. Come along to Fremont House for an interview tomorrow evening at 7pm, on the dot, to meet Burgatus Bulldog and the interview panel, as there is the possibility of an opening for you by way of a very interesting job at Fremont House, if you can put on a good show.'

Somewhat taken aback at this idea, but nonetheless having no desire to be negative, Albert blurted out, 'I shall be there, Deptus, make no mistake.' He was already puzzling over where he might find his old interview suit, which did, in a box somewhere, no doubt need a good airing, brush down and press if he was to make himself look at all well turned-out.

When Albert turned up half an hour early for his interview the following evening, Deptus hardly recognised him in his freshly pressed dark blue serge suit, white tailored shirt, highly polished boots and general first-class appearance. Albert's state of mind was rather like a stew pot boiling away on a stove: he felt all churned up and anxious that he might not be able to do his very best; luckily he calmed down in time for the in-depth interrogation for the job, which was undertaken by a panel of five seniors from the Residents Association and Burgatus Bulldog, who had patted him on the back for good luck when he arrived.

The questioning left no stone unturned, but Albert explained himself to the interviewers very well once he got going. Then, having been asked to wait outside the room while the panel had a short private discussion, it was not long before he was invited back in and told the good news. A job offer was made there and then which was accepted by a very excited Albert that very evening.

Albert was now immediately put on call at the Fremont House reception area in case of an emergency, but once a rota had been worked out, he was to regularly relieve Burgatus Bulldog for some day and night-time duties. It was to be a flexible arrangement with some time out to give variety and a pleasant lifestyle to those concerned. The arrangement was to be for a six-month probationary period to see how things panned out, but there was no doubt in anyone's mind that the scheme would run as smoothly as the cream on top of a trifle.

As Albert hurried home from his interview, he was seen by Hadden Hippo jumping in the air while banging his front paws together and whistling loudly!

Later that month, during one of Deptus' regular Friday evenings with the Bulldogs, they suggested to him that he was looking a little tired.

'Why don't you take a day off, Deptus?' said Burgatus Bulldog. 'Catch a coach and go for a good trip out of Dunlace? It will do you good to see some different surroundings and to breathe in some fresh invigorating air, as you have been working very hard just lately.'

Deptus thought about this and, knowing Burgatus and Belltring to be well-meaning and wise, he decided to take their advice. The very next morning, by way of encouragement, Belltring made Deptus some plump sardine sandwiches and prepared a flask of tea – and as a treat she included a large Bath bun in the picnic bag. There was nothing Belltring liked more than making up picnic lunches as she was a great enthusiast for eating outside in the open air whatever the weather (even if Burgatus had to wear his heavy overcoat). Deptus packed up his knapsack, put on his comfortable weekend shoes and newly purchased light windproof jacket with its matching cap, and made his way down to the coach station for an early start.

When he reached the station, he saw a coach heading to Landsmoth. He didn't know exactly where that was, although he understood that it was a good way out of the city of Dunlace and that it had some sound historical buildings, something that Deptus took a passing interest in. He bought his ticket, chose where to sit and plugged the in-ear headphones into his new BD4 player. Soon he was resting his head on the back of the comfy seat, casually looking out of the window, and tapping his paws to the beat of his favourite rock 'n' roll music.

The coach travelled along at a leisurely speed out of the city boundary and into the bright green countryside, peppered as it was with quaint and picturesque little villages.

8

The Day Trip

It was a warm sunny morning when the occupants of Waters-edge stirred from their beds. Daxham, who was always eager to go on an outing at the weekends, said he wanted to go to Landsmoth. As they all took their turn in choosing their destination, Daxham's wish settled the matter as it was his turn to pick.

Zig-Zag Pontoon rarely joined them on their trips out although he always included himself in the general discussion. Zig-Zag Pontoon hated shops of any kind (it reminded him of his visit to the garage-cum-convenience shop when he first made his escape from the factory) and as he never needed to buy any clothes or anything else for that matter, except perhaps an occasional tin of metal polish, he decided as usual to stay at home. By the time they were all ready to leave, Zig-Zag had already settled down in his favourite chair, and was busy connecting onto a new robotic app using their super high-grade top-performance communication device that Bardwell had recently bought from his favourite hi-tech internet site.

They didn't use Daxham's cart for any journeys as it always looked muddy and the tyres were usually half-flat, and although he was repeatedly told by Rilganna to hose it down and sort out the tyre pressures he never quite got the job started, always finding some annoying excuse to leave it until another time, which resulted in it never getting done at all.

As they could not all fit into one vehicle, they set off in two of their carts; Bardwell drove one and Peckleton the other. They soon made tracks to the park-and-ride transport station on the outskirts of Landsmoth where they could park up and catch one of the robotically guided hovering transporters which would take them straight to the rooftop of one of Rilganna's favourite stores in the city centre, Prittlewell & Tweasel.

Rilganna had her roomy shopping bag with her as she planned to buy some treats for their tea. She was also hoping to persuade Bardwell to buy a new pullover, which he was always reluctant to do as he liked his old ones, even if they were a bit tight and had a few holes in the sleeve. Bardwell was himself never all that keen on going out for the day as he much preferred to work at home on his computer, which he found much more interesting, especially when Daxham was occupied elsewhere, and he had some peace and quiet to concentrate without any disturbance. Bardwell always became completely immersed and single-minded once his machine was switched on and he got set on his plans for the day. On this occasion, though, he was persuaded to go out with them, as the weather was inviting and he felt in need of a change of scene after his week's work, which had been rather intense.

After a very short time Daxham became bored wandering around Prittlewell & Tweasel. He couldn't see any chance of buying himself anything as Bardwell was always telling him that he should put any spare money he had left in his pocket into his savings box, an opinion which Daxham considered to be the dullest and most uninteresting thing he had ever heard, so he decided to wander off on his own. He crossed the road and went towards Laurinston College, where he knew there was a nice old wall which at that time of the day was situated in full sunlight. He planned as usual to climb up onto it and watch the world go by as he sat enjoying the large strawberry flavoured ice cream, complete with a large chocolate flake sticking out at the top, that he had just bought from the little sweet shop on the corner.

As Daxham approached his favourite spot on the wall adjacent to the tall willowy beech hedge, he saw a large black cat eating a tempting-looking sandwich just where he normally sat. This, of course, was Deptus, who was tired after his sightseeing meanderings around Landsmoth and wanted some peace to sit and enjoy his refreshments in quiet composure. Daxham stared up at Deptus and as he thought he looked like an interesting character he immediately tried to engage him in conversation but received short shrift for his trouble. Daxham clambered up on the wall to sit alongside Deptus, at which point the large black cat growled and quickly moved further away. Daxham, taking absolutely no notice of the rebuff, followed Deptus as the now angry tourist tried again to put space between them.

'What have you got in your sandwich?' asked Daxham, holding his dripping ice cream cornet rather too near to Deptus' new windproof jacket. 'I must say it looks very tempting and tasty.'

'It's no business of yours, now buzz off,' said Deptus. This reply was quick and sharp, and the rest of it is not repeatable, but Daxham was never inclined to take a hint, however forcefully it was presented, and had no intention whatsoever of "buzzing off" – in fact he was not really quite sure what this meant.

Deptus got out his newspaper from his knapsack and held it close to his face, whereupon Daxham asked if he could read it too, explaining that Bardwell didn't encourage them to have a newspaper at the weekends since the prices went up.

Meanwhile the others still shopping in the store had suddenly noticed that Daxham was missing. This was always a concern, of course, but they had a good notion of where they might find him, and they were right. As they crossed the road, they could see that he was being as irritating as usual. Bardwell approached the large grumpy-looking black cat, sitting on the wall, with trepidation, but, being a brave badger, he held out a paw and introduced himself to Deptus. He apologised in such a genuinely decent way for Daxham's pushy behaviour that the large black cat offered his paw in return, and they cautiously made contact in this way.

Having introduced his companions to Deptus, Bardwell and he chatted together for some little while. There was without a doubt a friendly vibration between the two which was hard to fathom, especially as Deptus was suspicious of everyone, and always avoided social intermingling except with his longstanding Bulldog friends and a few others with whom he had the closest of relationships and trust. Deptus had good reason to be on his guard. Life was tough and he knew the trickery that stalked the world; he had seen more dodgy situations than he cared to recall and had trained himself to be grounded in reality, at all times. Deptus had no intention of ever losing his grasp in any situation, especially a new one, and caution in all things was his watchword.

Bardwell, wishing to prolong the pleasant interaction with Deptus, went on, 'I can only apologise once more for your lunch being disturbed by Daxham, who means well but whose manners are, more or less, non-existent. Here is my business card, and if ever you are around this way again, please do give us a call. We should all like to make your acquaintance more fully and instead of sardine sandwiches we shall dine together at Waters-edge; it would give us the greatest of pleasure.'

Deptus was becoming a trifle confused by all the unexpected attention so having climbed down from the wall he said a polite farewell to his new acquaintances and made his way back to the bus station. He had without a doubt experienced a very unusual and peculiar day: he was hot and bothered, was developing a nasty headache and just wanted to get back home to familiar surroundings. He found the coach that was going to the city of Dunlace, sat at the back of the vehicle and fell fast asleep until he reached his destination.

When he arrived back at Fremont House the Bulldogs were very pleased to see him, and Burgatus was keen to know all about his day's adventures.

Over a cup of chamomile tea, Deptus reflected on his

day's activities. He surprised himself with his enthusiasm as he began to tell the Bulldogs the whole story about how he had met a penguin, a badger, a lavender-coloured rabbit and a dog, and how very decent the badger had been and, thinking about it in retrospect, how funny the penguin was eating a huge ice cream cornet while sitting next to him on the wall. Burgatus listened with fascination and amused surprise as he heard all about the goings-on that Deptus had experienced.

Back in his apartment, Deptus stood Bardwell's business card on his shelf, went to bed and gradually forgot all about his adventures in Landsmoth, as he had some important matters to deal with during the forthcoming week and there was no time for daydreaming.

Some weeks went by and then one Saturday morning Belltring was helping Deptus with some chores – he always needed encouragement when it came to dusting and sweeping as cleaning up was one of his least favourite pastimes – when she chanced upon Bardwell's card on the shelf.

'Well,' she said, 'what's this?' and after hearing Deptus' explanation, Belltring said, 'Why not give this Bardwell a call? He seems to have been such a friendly badger and I'm sure his invitation was genuine, from what you said had happened on that Saturday at Landsmoth.'

Deptus couldn't do this, for he was self-conscious and reluctant when it came to communications involving social interaction. There was many an evening when he picked up his mobile with good intention and then put it down again, having made no progress at all, but the situation played on his mind and so on the next convenient Saturday he packed up his knapsack with a supply of food, that Belltring had given him the night before, and caught the train to Crindling village.

When he arrived, he got off the train and asked the station-keeper where Waters-edge was and received very clear instructions. He soon found the lane and the garden house, and then he just froze. What was he doing? He could hardly recognise himself in this embarrassing situation. He couldn't face knocking at the door and just as he was hurrying away and thinking how stupidly he was behaving Bardwell came along towards him, returning from a stroll, and they met face to face.

Bardwell immediately recognised Deptus and found seeing him quite overwhelming. He excitedly shook Deptus' paw while at the same time hugging him (rather too firmly). Bardwell called Rilganna and the others out to the front of the house and when they had recovered from the shock of seeing Deptus they all went back into Waters-edge together: Bardwell's arm remained firmly around Deptus' shoulder as he had no intention of letting him go.

Rilganna and Bardwell quickly prepared a tasty lunch using some of Peckleton's fresh produce from his vegetable patch, which went very nicely with Rilganna's mushroom flan, and Deptus' large packed lunch. Bardwell diplomatically enquired whether Deptus preferred to be called "Deptus" instead of "Dep", having started to call him the latter by mistake, and was informed that, as his friends called him Deptus or Dep, he didn't mind either name as he considered all at Waters-edge to be his new Crindling friends. Bardwell was delighted to hear this and so were the others, who all stood up and officially welcomed Deptus, clapping heartily!

Bardwell insisted that Deptus stay the night at Waters-edge and so he texted Burgatus to tell him that he would not be home until the following day. Burgatus heard of this new development with great pleasure.

'You enjoy yourself in Crindling,' return-texted kindly Burgatus Bulldog, 'for everything is good here, and Belltring sends her warmest wishes to everyone at Waters-edge.'

'What great news it is that Deptus is having a weekend of fun at long last,' said Belltring later. 'He is such a hardworking and conscientious cat and well deserves this change in his routine. Deptus always claims that he has been allotted a great number of tasks to carry out,' continued Belltring, who was never quite sure who or what drove Deptus on with such steely determination.

Next morning at Waters-edge, after a good night's sleep and a long-drawn-out and leisurely breakfast enjoyed by all at the big kitchen table, Peckleton proudly took Deptus on a tour of their large garden, closely shadowed by Zig-Zag Pontoon. The keen gardener eagerly explained all about the different plants, shrubs and vegetables in rather too much detail. Deptus did his best to show the right amount of interest when given in-depth information relating to the various types of peonies, campanula (bell-like flowers, explained Peckleton, when he saw Deptus looking a bit puzzled), roses, marigolds and bearded irises, which did not appear to have beards in the normal way of things, not to mention the propagation techniques favourable to courgettes and lettuces that could be relied on to increase their yield rate. Deptus was very impressed by Peckleton's knowledge and affection for all his plants although he felt his eyes gradually glazing over with so much detail to take on board, as it was still quite early in the morning.

Thankfully for Deptus, the walk-about finally ended and as all the friends sat together on the large log by the river, daydreaming in the sun, nonchalantly watching the dragonflies drifting on the breeze over the gently flowing water, Yaxlie Owl suddenly appeared from his headquarters to pass the time of day.

'Hi there, mateys,' he belted out loudly, half-frightening them to death, 'are you going to introduce me to your visitor, Bardwell? I always like to be acquainted with new arrivals to the neighbourhood.'

A formal introduction was soon satisfactorily carried out.

Coincidentally Hibberley Heron also arrived at about the same time and was his usual courteous self; however, he was as usual in a great hurry and too busy to stop for long. He was on his way to meet his friends at the gravel pits for a day's wading and a spot of sailing, a new hobby he had recently taken up, and was already running behind schedule, so in great haste he departed.

Later in the morning, Daxham, being as curious as ever, repeatedly asked Deptus what line of work he was in. It was hard for him to answer this question as his business dealings were numerous and not easily explained. In the end, Bardwell, using his natural perception and wisdom, replied to Daxham that Deptus was an entrepreneur. This explanation kept Daxham quiet for some considerable time, as he had to go indoors and clamber up the ladder to reach the top shelf in Bardwell's room, in order to access his large paper dictionary, the cover of which was rather dusty and made him sneeze not once, but numerous times as he struggled to get it down. Looking up this rather complicated word was not an easy task nor was checking it out on his e-dictionary, as he could not quite work out the first few letters to start him off, and so finally he gave up and went back outside to get a clue or two from the others, who couldn't help teasing him.

Sunday afternoon arrived far too quickly and so after a weekend of joy and discovery, and with fond farewells having been repeated many times over, Peckleton delivered Deptus to the train station in his cart and waved him off as the train disappeared along the track. They all agreed that Deptus was the most engaging cat they had ever met and the sooner he returned on a visit to Waters-edge the better it would be. Deptus had already promised to do just that.

In the last few months Deptus' life had changed beyond imagination. He had Burgatus and Belltring living close by him in their apartment, and what's more he now regularly saw his old friend Albert Alsatian since he had started his new job at Fremont House; and recently, due to an unexpected event, he had made five new friends whom he had to confess he was growing very fond of.

Deptus spent the entire train journey back to the city of Dunlace mulling over the happiness that these recent alterations to his lifestyle had brought about. The more he thought about the new situation, the more puzzled he became; fate was being unexpectedly kind to him, and it made him feel a trifle overwhelmed.

9

New Transport

It was late one afternoon, just after one of Deptus' weekend trips to Crindling, which were now a regular and much looked forward to event. He was in a relaxed mood and was whistling happily as he strolled along the bank of the River Rushmore, on his way back to Fremont House.

Suddenly his attention was drawn to a notice attached to Hadden Hippo's workshop building. It was a *For Sale* advertisement which read as follows:

Magatt car, Azure Blue, original condition; lightly used for its age. A good little runner – apply within.

Deptus knew that Hadden had a large and varied collection of vintage vehicles and so on impulse he rang the garage workshop's huge doorbell.

Burley Hadden Hippo, decked out in his working suit, opened the heavy double doors and immediately invited Deptus inside; he was surprised and pleased to see Deptus, as their paths hadn't crossed for a couple of weeks. Hadden showed Deptus the Magatt resting in the corner of his garage-cum-workshop, and at the same time they began catching up on local news. Hadden Hippo remarked on the great improvement he had seen in Albert Alsatian, who was his old vivacious self again and full of enthusiasm now he had his new job at Fremont House.

'I knew I could rely on you, Deptus,' said Hadden, patting him heartily on the back and shaking his paw for rather longer than was necessary, 'and guess what,' Hadden went on, 'Albert, in his quest to wipe out bad memories, has put his old red dressing gown and down-at-heel slippers into the disposable bin, so now they will vanish forever, never to reappear!'

It was great for them to see Albert so happily settled with a new purpose, and Burgatus Bulldog was also enjoying his new lifestyle with more free time. He now had more opportunity to work with Deptus on commercial ventures, which had a great spin-off as whenever the two friends bounced ideas off each other they invariably made good decisions.

Having looked over the old Magatt, Deptus was impressed and so they did a deal there and then over a cup of strong coffee and a good few of Hadden's favourite Garibaldi biscuits. Deptus recognised a good buy when he saw one, and Hadden made sure that it was a decent deal with a generous discount, as he had a lot of admiration for his old friend who had willingly done him many good turns over the years; in fact, so many that he couldn't remember them all, and now for once he had the chance to return a favour.

Hadden Hippo promised to give the old car a thorough once-over and a full service, followed by a good wash and polish. It was arranged that the Magatt was to be delivered direct to Waters-edge via a transporter during the coming week.

Bardwell was working away in his office at Waters-edge that Thursday morning and was at a crucial point in his calculations when he heard the gravel being noisily spun and crunched around outside. He peered through the window, and when he saw a huge transporter, complete with a car perched on the back, reversing onto the front driveway he ran to meet it and demanded its immediate removal, for no one at Waters-edge had ordered any kind of vehicle nor was expecting any such delivery. A heated argument ensued, and the frustrated driver climbed back into his cab and impatiently returned, showing Bardwell the paperwork with a signature on the bottom clearly signed *Deptus Dickens.* The residents of Waters-edge stood together on the gravel driveway staring at each other in complete astonishment.

Although the Waters-edge residents had their own carts, they were only spacious enough to hold the driver and two squashed-in passengers at any one time, which was not convenient when a day's jaunting out was planned, and Deptus had plenty of plans for those.

'Now at last we can all go out together in more comfort,' Deptus had muttered to himself when he had done the deal with Hadden Hippo.

Once they had recovered from the shock, Peckleton carefully positioned the Azure Blue Magatt car in the spacious wooden shed adjacent to Waters-edge and covered her over with a thick blanket, leaving her to rest in the tranquillity of the building after her long journey. Such pleasure did Deptus experience as all his friends squeezed together in front of the monitor screen to transmit their surprise and joy at the arrival of the Magatt; Deptus, too, was hardly able to control his own excitement. The pleasure of coming up with surprises was new to him but he was gradually getting used to it, and indeed as time went by Waters-edge and its residents found themselves the recipients of many interesting and fascinating items of eclectic taste that Deptus discovered during the course of his daily doings!

10

Lainstonbury-on-Sea and Windy Barn

Way out in the Quiverfell wilds was the quaint seaside town of Lainstonbury-on-Sea. This was where Deptus and the Waters-edge residents would sometimes go on a day's excursion in the Magatt if the weather was warm and sunny. They would enjoy a leisurely ride through the quiet country lanes with Bardwell at the wheel. Daxham invariably found the trips boring – he longed for some speed to pep things up, especially when they approached a very twisty bend, which offered the opportunity for some exciting action! There was, though, no chance of that happening with Bardwell at the wheel, so Daxham just yawned, sighed, and complained, while continuing to stare out of the window, usually munching the contents of a large bag of crisps.

Peckleton liked to visit Lainstonbury on Saturdays as there was a regular local market en route where he was able to buy more garden plants, a distraction that Daxham also found tedious and uninteresting, so he carried on grumbling when they stopped for Peckleton to buy the plants he liked the look of.

On this particular trip to Lainstonbury-on-Sea, they were walking along a narrow street in the town that they didn't normally frequent, having enjoyed morning drinks and cakes in the Corner Café, when Daxham stopped and stared up at a rather crestfallen wooden structure that was at the end of a row of old houses, to which it bore no resemblance in either style or construction. The old place was beginning to list precariously to one side and appeared to be the last remaining part of a decrepit two-tiered barn; the rest of the building having probably vanished due to neglect and the passage of time.

Daxham, turning to the others, suddenly said, 'That old place just whispered to me.'

All the others ignored this remark, because it was not unusual for Daxham to come up with bizarre exclamations at times, usually to get some attention. Just after Daxham had mentioned "the whisper", the old garden gate in front of the crooked path that led to the door of the old wooden building flew open, and they noticed a faded *For Sale* signboard, skewwhiff, and half hanging from its perch between the door and a dusty window; it was moving rhythmically backwards and forwards in the breeze while creaking at the same time.

Peering through the dirty windows it was clear that the wooden building was empty, and as they had already ascertained, was half-derelict and had probably been so for some considerable time. Bardwell, as was his usual habit, had been carefully saving up any bits of spare money they had left over after their bills had been paid and this nest-egg had grown into quite a decent fund. Recently he had been wondering whether they might spend the money on a worthwhile project – perhaps the renovation of an old building that needed some help – one that nobody else wanted to bother with. He thought that this would be an opportunity for them to learn new skills, have some fun together, and to see what they could achieve.

After they returned home to Waters-edge, Bardwell sat up late into the night with Deptus, mulling over the pros and cons of buying the old wooden structure. Together they checked out the Waters-edge finances, with Deptus offering to help out with any shortfall.

After making some enquiries the following day, Bardwell discovered that no conventional estate agent had managed to find a buyer for the old place and so it had recently been placed "for sale" with a firm that specialised in moving on "troublesome buildings". Bardwell made an immediate telephone call to the office of the specialist agent and an arrangement to view was set up for the following weekend.

Come the next Saturday, as Deptus and Bardwell were about to leave Waters-edge in the Magatt to embark on their journey of discovery, Daxham insisted on joining them, and made such a terrible fuss when they tried to put him off that they had no alternative but to take him along.

When they arrived at Lainstonbury-on-Sea to view the old property, they were met by the agent, a casually dressed and rather vague-looking llama, who eventually unlocked the front door, albeit with some difficulty, as the lock was rusty and stiff. In her attempt to gain access to the building the agent repeatedly dropped the key, restarting the process some four or five times over until she finally achieved success. When they eventually got inside, Bardwell and Deptus were taken aback to see how much work there was to do and how much dampness, dustiness and cobwebs lurked in dark dank corners.

Daxham, being his usual adventurous self, climbed up the two flights of rickety stairs ahead of the others until he reached the third floor, and made his way to the attic room, when something very odd happened. The loft door flew open and Daxham, curious as ever, went inside and then the door slammed firmly shut.

Miss Windy, who was the spirit of the old place, which was called Windy Barn, lived in the loft. She had a booming, dark brown voice and Daxham soon discovered that she was not one to be messed with.

'Look here, penguin, if that's what you are, as I can't say that you look like a typical example,' Miss Windy blurted out forcefully, well, actually, it was more aggressively than forcefully, 'there's only been one viewing since I was put up for sale and that was over three years ago and now you have turned up.'

It was indeed true that there had only been one viewing by a potential buyer. This was because he had heard such weird noises emanating from the attic space that he had taken fright, and because he had spread the word about locally that something malevolent was lurking in the property no one ever dared to go near it again.

Miss Windy continued with her story. 'No one has actually lived in my rooms for five years, and I'm being ignored and what's more, I'm full of unflattering dust and dampness. Being a figment of fun and ridicule along the street is no walk in the park and I am badly out of sorts and depressed. I sincerely hope your friends will take me on and make me look smarter than all those other spiteful "monstrosities" in the nearby row. Now don't you let me down: I shall be listening and watching your efforts, and be sure, I don't take prisoners.'

Daxham was overwhelmed with panic and terrified witless, but he promised Miss Windy that he would do his very best to positively influence Bardwell and Deptus towards a sale, just to get out of the loft, the door to which banged loudly shut once he had made his escape. Daxham almost fell over his own feet as he hurried away, so shaken was he by the experience.

'You look very shocked,' Bardwell remarked when Daxham arrived at the bottom of the wonky old stairs, having travelled at a great turn of speed. 'What's the matter? Your beak has turned quite pale.'

Once Daxham had got his breath back, he said in a flurry, 'I really like this old wooden place, Bardwell.'

'Well, we're not too sure about the whole idea,' said Bardwell and Deptus together, clearly of the same opinion, 'for there will be a lot of arduous work to be done to make it look anything like decent and let's face it, it's such an unsightly eyesore in the neighbourhood, for want of a better description, and that's being polite about it. Why on earth are you so keen on it?'

Daxham refrained from making any kind of reply and hoped Miss Windy hadn't been listening, as she would have been very offended by the aforementioned description proffered by Bardwell and Deptus, and for once Daxham was lost for words.

To cut a long story short, in the end, and after much debate and deliberation, not to mention fluctuating indecision, the residents of Waters-edge and Deptus decided to embark on the venture, feeling that a challenge would not be a bad thing. What a relief this was for Daxham, who was receiving daily text messages via Miss Windy's huge cobweb-covered mobile phone, urging him on, and now at last he was able to send a positive return text to her regarding the purchase of old Windy Barn by the residents of Waters-edge and Deptus.

Once they had acquired the dilapidated old place, they frequented it as often as they could, as they tried to puzzle out where to begin to put it right. At weekends, when the weather was clement, as Windy Barn was rather draughty and damp, they camped overnight, on makeshift beds that Zig-Zag made up for them, as he was skilful at putting temporary structures together at great speed.

At last, having thought through the project, they agreed that there was much modification and restructuring work to be done and so a builder with a special interest in dilapidations and carpentry was needed. Seeing an advertisement in the local newspaper, the *Lainstonbury Lantern*, they telephoned for the owner of a local building firm, who seemed to be a suitable contender for the job, to call on them to discuss the work.

The following week they were back again at Windy Barn, awaiting the arrival of the builder, who turned out to be a rather dapper-looking hedgehog, smartly dressed in a tweedy sort of way. He had an impolite manner about him and his attitude when dealing with them was one of dismissive impatience: it was as if he was in a terrible hurry and had no intention of hanging around wasting time on them. He looked about him and soon sorted out what was needed, and with a few scribbles on his notepad gave a price there and then, having more or less ignored any comments or opinions put forward by the keepers of Windy Barn and in fact he barely acknowledged their presence.

In addition to supporting the listing structure so that it didn't continue its journey "downwards", the proposal involved demolishing the old leaky wooden outhouse on the front and replacing it with something similar but waterproof; the installation of new windows, cupboards, and a garden fence; a new path was also required, as well as other miscellaneous items, all of which Mr Finningham Hedgehog took account of, or so they hoped.

Just as Bardwell was about to say that they would need to obtain a comparative price and that he would be in touch again soon, Mr Finningham Hedgehog, as if reading Bardwell's mind, suddenly said, 'Take it or leave it. You certainly won't find a better builder around here or be offered a keener price. If you don't trust me with the job, then you can please yourselves. I have plenty of other work on my books.'

Completely shocked by this forthright outburst they looked at each other in disbelief.

Having put his pen back in his prickly top where he got it from, Finningham Hedgehog took himself off through the front door and climbed back into his blue truck, and without looking back, drove away without any further conversation or niceties having been expressed, and that was the end of that.

By then it was late in the afternoon and as they were all feeling jaded by the experience of dealing with the builder and his rather truculent attitude, not to mention his sweeping decisions, they decided to travel back to Waters-edge in leisurely style in the old Magatt, spending the journey time in reflective silence.

Once back at Waters-edge, they looked at some testimonials on Finningham Hedgehog's website and Deptus, who had a connection in the area (he seemed to have them everywhere), made a call on his mobile and received from his contact the most glowing of references regarding the company of Finningham Hedgehog, Daughters, Sons, Nieces and Nephews.

Although it went against Bardwell's better judgement, as he had no other comparable quotation, which resulted in his enduring a sleepless night, he was persuaded by the others to telephone the builder the next day to accept the price for the work, which was scheduled to commence a month or two ahead.

And what a task it turned out to be: cutting out damp and rotting timbers and rebuilding part of the wooden structure, scraping, making good, and painting; it was quite an undertaking and they all joined in. Peckleton mapped out a kind of campaign plan for them all to follow, and after a few weeks, things started to take shape in a positive way. Daxham, meanwhile, had become very close to Miss Windy. As soon as he arrived, he would hasten upstairs and into the attic as the loft door flew open, which was then quickly secured once Daxham was safely inside. If any of the others tried to gain entry it remained firmly closed.

Talking to Finningham Hedgehog one day, Rilganna told him how worried she was about Daxham conversing with himself in the attic. Finningham, looking directly at

Rilganna, said, 'Story has it that the spirit of the old place lives in the attic, apparently a harmless but very cantankerous individual. If she has befriended Daxham there is nothing to worry about.'

'Well, I hope you are right,' replied Rilganna, who was not completely content with the explanation she had received. She decided there and then not to dwell on the subject, but thought it best nonetheless to tell the others about it just in case something mysterious happened to Daxham, as he had absolutely no judgement about anything he ever did or said.

Daxham listened closely to Miss Windy's fascinating reminiscences about the carryings-on in Victorian times, for Windy Barn had been converted into a dwelling in 1887. As it turned out, it was all that remained of an ancient flour mill. Miss Windy had resided in the loft area at Windy Barn since 1887, having been cruelly turned out from the attic room of an old Virginia creeper-covered manor house where she had previously lived for decades. She had been blamed for some unexplained nastiness in the property, about which she said she knew absolutely nothing. She was adamant that this was the malicious work of a new incumbent who had set about destroying her good name in a plan to take over her space in the attic, and Miss Windy had been down on her luck ever since then. Daxham looked at her sympathetically, as he thought that might be the best thing to do.

Miss Windy had a memory like no other and Daxham listened carefully to her stories. He refused to divulge anything he heard from her to any of the others as that was his promise to her, and Daxham certainly didn't want to get wrong-footed against such a formidable force. They were all astonished by the laughter they could hear echoing out from the loft and they could not help wondering what tales Daxham might be making up, probably about them, as he had a wild and vivid imagination and had a habit of getting over-excited and showing off when he was trying to make a good impression.

Miss Windy had inherited an old mahogany radiogram in 1953, together with a vintage collection of "78" records that had been discarded by a previous owner of Windy Barn when he left. She would proudly play some of her old records for Daxham to listen to. Sometimes he was allowed to choose the music for their evening's entertainment, although he had to be very careful, as the records were made out of something called shellac resin, which he had never heard of, and were easily broken, which made him nervous as he tended to be accident prone. He had to concentrate very hard, especially as Miss Windy always kept an unwavering eye on what he was doing, which made him more jumpy than he might otherwise have been.

Playing records further cemented Miss Windy and Daxham's friendship and they became musical companions. Daxham accompanied Miss Windy in her singing once he had learnt the words of the songs, which at first were unfamiliar to him, although he found the lyrics easy to remember once he was practised and got the hang of them.

'Oh dear,' said Bardwell one evening, 'how long is it going to be before Daxham gets fed up with singing along to Miss Windy's records? It rather reminds me of an out-of-tune foghorn going off on a dark eerie night: I shall have to buy some ear plugs if this noise goes on for much longer!'

The firm of Finningham Hedgehog, Daughters, Sons,

Nieces and Nephews did exemplary work, and although there were heaps of dust, mess and old lumps of wood here, there and everywhere, and some trepidation when the younger members of the hedgehog team banged a great hole in a wall looking for an old fireplace that had been blocked up and plastered over years earlier, everything worked out smoothly. Daxham, who watched with interest as the frowsty, old, plastered wall was being partially demolished, got completely covered in soot, dust and cobwebs as it suddenly revealed its secrets. The hedgehogs laughed and laughed when they saw Daxham looking so dirty and dusty, as he was very good at giving advice about things he knew absolutely nothing about, and regularly got in their way when they were working.

It took many more weeks of effort before the old structure was looking good. Miss Windy, who was delighted by her new appearance, refused to talk with any of the other houses in the nearby row that had made fun of her in the past; whatever they did she refused to be friends. She turned her newly built brick chimney stack away whenever she was approached in conversation, and waited patiently all week long, hoping for a visit from her new keepers. Once she saw the old Azure Blue Magatt being parked up in the back yard, she would unlock the loft door in the attic, ready to greet her most favourite friend and visitor. In fact, she never had any other callers, as she was unsociable and scared off all-comers without exception. If a couple of weekends went by without any action, Miss Windy would bellow loudly down her mobile at Daxham, demanding his swift appearance.

Soon the little front garden at Windy Barn was filled with colourful flowers at every season of the year. The uneven and broken paving stones had been removed, and in their place Peckleton planted a soft chamomile lawn for them to rest their picnic blanket on during long summer days spent outside.

11

Zig-Zag Pontoon's Robotic AI Boost

Deptus was becoming increasingly concerned about Zig-Zag Pontoon's predicament. Although he never grumbled and seemed happy enough, the restrictions he had to endure were a burden. He was unable to go anywhere unless he was sure that he could have easy access to a power point, the arrangements for which did not always go to plan.

Deptus had recently read an article in a learned journal he had found on a train when he was travelling to an activity trail event. He had been given a free ticket for the event but when he arrived at the destination, he was quite out of his comfort zone, so he was soon on the way home again! This article was about a robotic specialist who worked in the Experimental Robotics Department at the city of Dunlace's Central University, who claimed to be able to fit-up a permanent power supply by means of a small powerful

AI battery booster into the internal workings of some small robots, so that they never need think about power sockets ever again.

It sounded a tricky procedure, but Deptus decided nonetheless to telephone the department to find out more about the possibilities for Zig-Zag Pontoon.

After hearing about Zig-Zag's predicament from Deptus Dr Waffle-Zippity, the AI battery booster expert, made room in his busy schedule to see Zig-Zag within the next fortnight. This meant that Zig-Zag Pontoon had to make the trip to the city of Dunlace to stay in the visitor's apartment at Fremont House, in order to keep his appointment. Deptus worked out that Zig-Zag's battery would just about last the duration of the train journey from Crindling to Dunlace and if he was plugged into a power socket immediately on his arrival at Fremont House all would be well.

Deptus explained to Zig-Zag what he had found out from Dr Waffle-Zippity and that the opportunity for a discussion was there, if Zig-Zag wanted to take it up. It turned out that the little robot was enthusiastic about meeting with Dr Waffle-Zippity, so a date was fixed.

The journey for Zig-Zag down to Fremont House went uneventfully and upon his arrival he soon settled in and began to enjoy his stay. He quickly became the centre of attention and met up with just about everyone, including Hadden Hippo, who called by each day to see him. The close attention that Zig-Zag received did not take away the uneasy feelings of butterflies he had in his workings and when it came to the day of the assessment at the medical centre Zig-Zag was nervously excited. With Albert driving them, in Burgatus Bulldog's city vehicle, Deptus and Zig-Zag arrived in good time, to meet with Dr Waffle-Zippity, at the University's Department of Experimental Robotics.

The specialist, who was very interested to discuss Zig-Zag's plight, explained that if he turned out to be a suitable candidate (of particular importance was whether Zig-Zag's previously installed trial AI chip, expressed enough appropriate autonomous robotic signs to make the procedure plausible) he could install his newly designed powerful AI battery booster into Zig-Zag's workings. The patient would then have a state-of-the-art permanent power source and if the procedure worked out well, Zig-Zag could forget all about power sockets forever. This was just what Deptus and Zig-Zag wanted to hear.

During the consultation, Dr Waffle-Zippity poked and prodded Zig-Zag and asked him all kinds of questions about his wiring, which Zig-Zag didn't know much about, although he was able to report that a trial chip had been installed inside his workings at the factory, enabling him to have a good degree of "independent AI thinking". This information, apparently, made Zig-Zag an excellent candidate, and so, with this positive news in mind, it was decided that the procedure to transplant one of Dr Waffle-Zippity's permanent powerful AI battery boosters into his robotic system could be carried out two days later, as Dr Waffle-Zippity had an unexpected gap in his schedule and was keen to get on with the job.

Deptus felt sure that long-term this was the right course of action for Zig-Zag Pontoon so that he could lead a happier, less restricted life without the anxiety of having to locate power sockets. Although Zig-Zag was quite excited by this new prospect, he was nevertheless a little reticent: at the back of his mind he had a terror of something going wrong and ending up back at the awful factory again. The night before his follow-up appointment to see Dr Waffle-Zippity, Zig-Zag remained wide awake… and so did Deptus.

When Zig-Zag, Deptus and Albert arrived at the University, they parked up in a specially allocated parking area, and were soon greeted by the specialist who was on schedule to undertake the procedure. After completion of some obligatory paperwork Zig-Zag was fitted up with an oversized white medical gown, and it all began to look rather clinical. Dr Waffle-Zippity's assistant escorted Zig-Zag Pontoon into the installation area of the Experimental Robotics Department and so the work began.

Deptus and Albert, having said farewell to Zig-Zag, sat together in the waiting area unable to hide their concern. Once the action started, they could hear the movement of metal instruments and the clicking and clunking of paraphernalia. After about an hour the lights and the noisy machinery in the installation theatre area suddenly failed. A persistent high-pitched emergency warning siren issued out, with no sign of reducing its volume. In the treatment room, Dr Waffle-Zippity was in a most urgent state of mind; his face had turned completely white, and he was sweating profusely. He could not resuscitate poor Zig-Zag, who had taken a turn for the worse, and was turning rusty in front of the team's very eyes.

They all feared the most dreadful of outcomes and poor Deptus when he heard the news felt a terrible burden of regret. It had all gone so terribly wrong.

All of a sudden, after a disheartening pause which lasted for about five minutes, Zig-Zag suddenly came to life: the rust quickly disappeared from his handsome exterior and his eyes were flashing brighter than ever. With a loud clatter he was able to get himself up and mobile. His new permanent AI battery booster that had been attached within his workings by Dr Waffle-Zippity had suddenly powered up and the small external aerial attached to the top of his head was making a blissful whirring noise. The whole team started to cheer loudly, and Deptus and Albert joined in, giving Zig-Zag a great hug and Dr Waffle-Zippity a hefty bang on his back by way of congratulation.

Unfortunately, these feelings of elation and relief did not last for long. After a few minutes, Zig-Zag's systems went into free fall: the little robot recognised no one familiar and was set on a path that was terrifying to see. Ignoring all in his midst and defying capture, he marched through the University's reception area and out into the street. He was on an unstoppable pathway back to the factory that had produced him; a calamity was in their midst.

Deptus was furious with Dr Waffle-Zippity.

'You fool!' he shouted. 'You have ruined Zig-Zag's life and now we have to stop him returning to the robot factory.'

Dr Waffle-Zippity was annoyed with himself. He had not envisaged such a serious incompatibility to arise between his permanent powerful AI battery booster and Zig-Zag's original trial AI chip and wiring, which had been fitted into his workings at the factory. Zig-Zag's mechanisms were now seriously compromised. Although Dr Waffle-Zippity had known that the experimental procedure was a risky prospect, he had nonetheless decided that it was worth a calculated chance. As it turned out, the default system, that was programmed to lead Zig-Zag back to the factory where he had been created, had not been neutralised as he had hoped;

instead it had been triggered and nothing could be done to stop poor Zig-Zag's inevitable journey to destruction.

Deptus was overwhelmed by grief and guilt, but he was a warrior, and was not going to give up on Zig-Zag that easily.

He grabbed his mobile and hastily tried to contact Hadden Hippo. Hadden often wore his ear defenders when he was using noisy equipment in his workshop and could not always hear the buzzing of incoming calls on his phone. Deptus telephoned Burgatus Bulldog, who hastened round to Hadden's workshop to ask him to contact Deptus posthaste.

Hadden Hippo was a senior member of the Voluntary Security Brigade and if anyone could help in this emergency, he could. Hadden listened to the story and then he replied, 'This is a horror story, Deptus, make no mistake. Do you know the whereabouts of Zig-Zag Pontoon at this moment?'

'He's on the way back to the factory, where he will be destroyed,' replied Deptus, words tumbling out in jagged breathless bursts.

'Leave this to me,' said Hadden, 'let me think for a few minutes.' Before too long Hadden had an idea of sorts; whether it would work or not was unpredictable, but they had to give it a go.

Meanwhile Zig-Zag Pontoon was stomping along the pathways, over roads in front of vehicles, pushing his way onto buses and being just about as single-minded as a determined robot can get.

It was not long before Hadden Hippo managed to sight Zig-Zag Pontoon on his Voluntary Security Brigade monitor: he alerted the Voluntary Armoured Truck Division and with their highly sensitive navigation devices now working to full capacity, Zig-Zag's exact position was traced. A double-skinned armoured truck with its huge blast-proof doors now wide open was parked in Zig-Zag's path by the skilled volunteer operators. In due course Zig-Zag walked straight into the truck, and the doors automatically shut. Zig-Zag was now enclosed and there was no way he was going any further.

Deptus was relieved that Zig-Zag had been stopped in his robotic steps, but this was a dangerous situation. The procedure that Dr Waffle-Zippity had carried out had proved disastrous. Zig-Zag could not spend forever in the back of an armoured truck; for the moment there was stalemate and very little time to think.

From the workstation viewings transmitted from inside the truck the volunteer operators could see that Zig-Zag, desperate to get out, was still trying to push himself forward. He was biffing himself up against the inside of the truck, badly damaging his metalwork, such that his wiring was starting to poke out. Finally, he fell down. Zig-Zag was no more: he lay there as dead as a doorstop.

The doors of the armoured truck were speedily opened up, and Zig-Zag's metal remains were removed from the vehicle by experts from the Armoured Truck Division. In no time at all they were quickly on their way back to the University by motorbike despatch rider in a stout plastic bag. It was sad to see the little robot's bright metalwork rapidly rusting and there was not a glimmer of life in any part of his being.

As soon as Zig-Zag's parts arrived at the University, they were hurried into the Experimental Robotic Department's intensive care unit. Dr Waffle-Zippity, with his team gathered around him, pulled down the shutters of the unit and the door was secured. An intermittent emergency red light flashed on and off at monotonous intervals.

Dr Waffle-Zippity's international reputation was on the line and the press were now onto the story. A remote international conference was underway and Dr Waffle-Zippity was surrounded by his most geeky technical experts and experimental robotic specialists.

The concentration in the intensive care unit was red-hot and the windows were steaming up in spite of the air conditioning system working at full strength. Zig-Zag Pontoon was completely dismantled, his wiring was disentangled and his workings, resembling a spaghetti junction, were in a pile on a low trestle table, but things were happening. It took five hours of intricate and delicate wiring before Zig-Zag Pontoon was finally put together again. All his old factory microchips had been removed and he was rebuilt from scratch. He was now lying flat out on a stretcher with a large flexible pipe connecting him to all manner of artificial intelligence support machines; the next few hours were critical.

Albert was doing his very best to console Deptus while they sat in the waiting area, but Deptus was devastated. Although he was angry with Dr Waffle-Zippity, he knew in his heart of hearts that it had been his fault for suggesting the procedure in the first place and, hard though Albert tried, he could not console Deptus and settle down his feelings of remorse.

After about an hour, Dr Waffle-Zippity came out of the AI transfer room, an offshoot of the intensive care unit, where Zig-Zag was now placed, and walked slowly across the corridor towards Deptus and Albert sitting in the waiting room. Just as he was starting to explain about the uphill struggle that still lay ahead of them, an intensive care assistant hurried across the corridor from the unit, declaring that Zig-Zag's aerial was beginning to quietly and slowly whirl round and hum; at last there were positive signs of life.

It took several days but Zig-Zag made a sound recovery. Of course, he had no memory of the trauma that had happened to him, because he had been completely rebuilt, but he looked and felt wonderful. There was no risk of his ever finding his way back to the factory again because that risky section of his circuitry had been killed off and removed. He was now a fully operational free-thinking robot, and what's more he would never need a power socket again. Dr Waffle-Zippity and his team had learned a lot from their recent experience and their reputation soared. Dr Waffle-Zippity was rewarded for his trend-setting work when he was conferred with the title of Professor of Powerful Battery Boosters with regard to Small Robots by the eminent University, and a whole new raft of research papers were spawned as a result of Dr Waffle-Zippity and his team's achievements in reassembling Zig-Zag Pontoon's mechanisms and workings.

Miraculously, although Zig-Zag had undergone an immensely complicated reassembling procedure that he had no memory of, Dr Waffle-Zippity and his team had managed to safeguard Zig-Zag's memory recall from before his crash and astonishingly he was able to remember all his friends and most of his past life, including his production at the factory and his momentous escape.

All at Waters-edge and Fremont House had been taking turns to wait by their centralised mobile phone device for updates about Zig-Zag's progress: they had not been able to do very much productive work of late as they were paralysed by gloomy imaginings which were running wild between them. When at last they heard the wonderful news that Deptus and Zig-Zag Pontoon were on their way back to Waters-edge in the University's medical support vehicle, they were overjoyed, and Daxham was allowed two large bottles of ginger beer to celebrate.

Zig-Zag was so relieved to be going back to Waters-edge, that as he arrived on a portable bed, tears began to fall down his metal front when he saw all his friends waiting for him. He was very tired and slept soundly all night long under his favourite quilt and for the first time in his life he knew that when he woke up, he didn't need to be anywhere near a power socket!

Zig-Zag Pontoon spent his convalescence period exploring the countless automatically updating devices and apps now available to him via his new powerful AI battery booster attachment. He was linked to the latest trends and all manner of worldwide entertainment facilities, which he could access on the University's newly developed experimental HD fully operational electronic tube connection set, sent to him courtesy of Dr Waffle-Zippity's department. Slowly but surely, Zig-Zag got back his full strength and energy, and was his contented self once more.

It was not unusual for Daxham to shout at least four times a day, 'Three cheers for Zig-Zag, Deptus and Dr Waffle-Zippity!' until everyone got completely tired of hearing the repetitive message. Deptus gradually recovered from the anxiety that he had experienced, although he rather suspected that the stress he had recently been under might have reduced his lifespan by at least two cat years and it took some time for his normally optimistic attitude to return to him.

12

Rilganna's New Tooth and Albert's Opportunity

Rilganna was conscientious when it came to the care of her teeth, brushing away at them three times a day using her motorised toothbrush, which was good for getting into tight corners. Unlike other rabbits of a more conventional type, Rilganna's teeth didn't continue growing and replacing themselves, so she knew she would only ever have one set of teeth and as eating was one of her favourite pastimes, she fiercely safeguarded their wellbeing by attending regular appointments for dental checks at the clinic not far away from home.

At Rilganna's recent examination the junior partner who initially checked over her teeth referred her to the senior dentist, Mr Scammondi Squirrel, but not before she had read out the following diatribe from a cue card.

'Mr Scammondi Squirrel has just obtained a brand-new

ingenious robotic machine, a kind of magical robotic tooth implant device, which automatically extracts problem teeth and then redesigns and produces replica ones to any size and shape in existence. In fact, the whole procedure is just like magic. The machine is the first in Glenland to be used at a dental clinic and has been a most expensive financial commitment for Mr Scammondi Squirrel. You have a dental problem, Rilganna, which ideally fits into the category of requiring a robotic tooth implant.'

At the end of the speech Rilganna was not quite sure what to do but her indecision went unnoticed and at the speed of light she was booked into the following day's appointments system to see Mr Scammondi Squirrel for an assessment.

'You will need a tooth replacement, as one has become badly cracked and damaged, and as no other remedial treatment is suitable I shall need to activate my new automatic robotic tooth implant device to rectify the problem,' confirmed an exuberant Mr Scammondi Squirrel the next day.

As Bardwell had managed to accumulate a few more additional funds since their project was finished in Lainstonbury-on-Sea, an appointment for the hi-tech robotic dental work was arranged for the following Tuesday. There was unease in the back of Rilganna's mind that she could not quite understand, but she decided to put her reticence down to "fear of the unknown".

***

Come the day of the appointment, the dental experience for Rilganna turned out to be pretty extraordinary, not to mention futuristic. Mr Scammondi Squirrel assisted the brightly painted emerald-green robotic device into the consulting room. The contraption was single-minded, and once it had received instructions via a robotic keypad from its keeper, in this case Mr Scammondi Squirrel, it acquired the essential measurements and information it needed to produce the required replacement tooth, while simultaneously extracting the original one. The device whistled, shook, banged and shuffled about in a purposeful, businesslike manner, until eventually out popped a brand-new tooth which nicely replaced Rilganna's original one in both design, colour and appearance; it was then fitted by the robotic machine in no time at all.

Mr Scammondi Squirrel, wearing a highly decorative bright green waistcoat, that matched almost to perfection the colour of his new robotic tooth implant device, proudly puffed out his chest as he danced around showing Rilganna the newly replicated tooth in a mirror.

With the job having been completed, the robotic device chugged itself away into a corner and went into its resting position. As Rilganna's appointment was the last of the day, Mr Scammondi Squirrel pushed down the robot's tall protruding aerial and covered the device over with a large green plastic hood which had a wide elastic band sewn along the bottom to keep it in position. The activity made Rilganna recall a parrot she once knew who lived in the park. He closed down his quarters in much the same way as dusk descended and it was time for him to go to bed.

With Bardwell and Rilganna having paid the rather large bill they left the dental clinic and returned to Waters-edge, content in the knowledge that she now had a strong, newly replaced tooth.

*　*　*

Albert was resting in his sitting room after a day's duties at Fremont House, watching one of his favourite programmes on his television which had an elongated fully digitised screen, when there was a sharp knock at the front door. Albert, who was not expecting any callers, went to see who was there and was very surprised to find the manager of Blisk & Blofells, where he used to work as the store's senior detective before he injured his leg on his cycling holiday all that time ago, standing in front of him. Albert invited Mr Hockerill Hearthrug, a very smart goat, into his newly painted sitting room and offered him a mug of hot chocolate and a slice of buttered toast.

'It is very good to see you again,' said Mr Hearthrug, accepting the offer of refreshments and taking a seat at Albert's invitation, 'and looking so well, too. I can see that your leg has been restored to good health. I have come along to offer you your old job back as chief store detective. The incidence of shoplifting has gone up alarmingly at Blisk & Blofells since you vacated your post and, quite honestly, your replacement is simply not up to the job. Within the boundaries of common sense, you can name your conditions and dictate your salary.'

Albert was rather surprised (and not a little flattered), as anyone would have been at this invitation, but he knew what his reply had to be. He was not the kind of Alsatian who was much bothered about money. After all, what was he going to spend the extra funds on? He had gone off cycling, and that was not about to change, and in any case, he had recently sold his racing bike as it kept getting in his way, as it was awkwardly stored in his passageway. He didn't want to move out of his apartment to a bigger space as he was very comfortable where he was and liked being close to his old friend, Hadden Hippo. Albert always enjoyed their conversations together, and he regularly helped Hadden out with his bills in his spare time, as he found paperwork very bothersome, and Albert certainly didn't want to disappoint him.

He didn't need any new outfits as his clothes cupboard was full to exploding as his stock never seemed to wear out, and above all how ungrateful would he be if he let Deptus, Burgatus and Belltring down when they were always so kind to him. In addition to that, he had become very fond of all the cat families who lived in Fremont House and although they were dubious of him at first, as his appearance was rather large and furry, he was pretty sure they liked him now, judging by the great number of bulldog flags, homemade greeting cards, multi-coloured balloons, boxes of chocolates, raspberry jam doughnuts, home-knitted paw socks and dog magazines he had received from them all on the occasion of his recent birthday.

'I am grateful, Mr Hearthrug, for your calling here to see me with this generous offer,' said Albert, 'but I am content and happy with my life now and I have a new career. Although my leg looks healed it might let me down if I run about on it too much so I will have to decline returning to Blisk & Blofells.'

'Now don't be too hasty, Albert,' Mr Hearthrug went on, engaging a more determined tone. 'I will return next week, and I am sure that by then you will have changed your mind when you have thought on the matter for a few days.'

'Really, please don't come back again,' said Albert, adopting an equally firm and definite manner, 'as I have no intention of changing my mind and I really don't want the bother of a further discussion on the subject. It is decent of you to think of me, and I know that at the time of my accident you found me an alternative post in the basement at Blisk & Blofells to keep me going, which I appreciated at the time although it didn't work out for me, but my life has completely changed now, and it would be a big mistake to go back over old ground.' Albert continued, without a pause, 'I enjoy the various duties involved in my new job. No day or week is identical. I can be trimming rose bushes in the Fremont House garden one day, and then, with my wide knowledge of local history from my tour guide days, I can be escorting visitors and clients around the city of Dunlace for Deptus Dickens a day later. This is quite apart from my various reception, security, and maintenance duties, all of which I very much enjoy, and above all I am totally committed to the wellbeing and safety of all the cat residents at Fremont House.' Having finished his diatribe, Albert was relieved to take a deep breath.

With this final statement having sunk in, and having abandoned acceptance of the refreshments, the disappointed goat got up to leave, shaking Albert's paw and wishing him farewell and good luck. Albert didn't have half a second's doubt that his decision had not been the right one and was greatly relieved when he had shut the door on Mr Hearthrug and he had gone away, enabling Albert to forget all about the unsettling suggestion that he could well have done without.

13

The Annual Celebrations

The celebration of the annual Honey Oak Friday and Supersonic Year Day came and went and there was much excitement in the air.

Deptus arrived at Waters-edge on Honey Oak Friday looking well turned out in a new cardigan, which had rather exaggerated wide stripes, that Albert had found for him in the sales. He was laden with gifts for all his friends, all parcelled up and tied securely with coloured string.

Earlier and on the spur of the moment, Peckleton had bought a huge flowering shrub from the nearby garden centre. Although it was colourful and seasonal it was quite unsuitable, as it was too tall and too wide to get over the threshold and into Waters-edge. They had to push and shove with all their strength until finally, with patience and much trimming of its sprouting greenery, it was eventually eased into their living room.

While this activity was going on Rilganna was quietly recalling less happy times when she lived at the Ultor Commune. The Elderians always left a pile of surprise packages on Supersonic Year Day morning for resident Ultorians and she would rummage hopefully through, but there had never been one left for her. She always worked hard, making chocolate decorations, and preparing celebration food, and felt meanly treated as no one ever thanked her. Happily, those dreadful memories were more distant now that she had a more cheerful new life, but sometimes, when she least expected it, they would still trickle back into her mind from her memory bank and cause her unhappiness.

Rilganna was persuaded by Daxham to help him decorate the unwieldy shrub with paper flowers and colourful make-believe birds which were timed by tiny batteries to tweet and whistle at regular intervals; this involved encouraging her to climb to the top of the enormous plant. He then mischievously moved the ladder from beneath her so there she was, stuck up in the air, perilously hanging onto the thick foliage. He was in deep trouble for his inconsiderate behaviour, and as Rilganna's rage worsened, the more photographs Daxham took of her anger, using the camera on his new mobile phone which Deptus had given him for his birthday. Once Rilganna was restored to ground level, it took quite some time for the heat of this debacle to settle down and peace to be restored, which fortunately occurred in time for the celebrations to be enjoyed without a nasty atmosphere hovering over their activities.

It was with some reluctance that Rilganna accepted Daxham's "heartfelt" apology but with it came the condition that all the photographs of her caught in this awkward predicament, which were stored in Daxham's mobile phone, were to be permanently removed, so that they could not be restored and displayed on their HD television monitor for all to see, which was one of his more annoying tricks.

The following day was Supersonic Year Day. Deptus had a business opportunity to explore in the morning with Burgatus Bulldog in the city of Dunlace, so he had to return to Fremont House late on Honey Oak evening, but the others all went to Windy Barn in the blue Magatt, much to the delight of Miss Windy.

Daxham spent most of his time in the attic room in the loft, having taken his sandwiches, cakes, and ginger beer upstairs on a tray. The others appreciated this break from Daxham's endless chattering and exasperating behaviour as it could be quite exhausting. They did, though, have to put up with him singing along to Miss Windy's favourite songs, that as usual rang out loud and clear from the loft, no more in tune than usual.

Back at Enterprise Wharf, the final arrangements for the annual Supersonic Year Day evening party planned for the residents of Fremont House, scheduled to start at 8pm, were underway.

A generous buffet had been ordered from Lucy's, a favourite delicatessen of theirs in Ruddle Lane. The delivery van carrying the tempting treats coincided with the return of Deptus and Burgatus from their business negotiations. The previous week Deptus had ordered a three-tiered, richly fruited honey cake from Patricia's Patisserie in Rapid Row, which was to be decorated with brightly coloured candles: in fact these were mini indoor cake sparklers doubling up as neat little candles that ignited with a minute's warning once lit, and promised to burst forth with vivid fountains of colour.

The tempting array of food was spread out in the front reception area of Fremont House on a trestle table normally used for wallpapering, but it looked great now that it was covered with a huge red and yellow paper tablecloth. Fresh flower decorations that Belltring had spent a long time designing and making were displayed in strategic places between large dishes and plates full of tasty indulgencies.

Albert had spent all morning fixing a long row of large confetti-filled balloons all the way up the staircase sides, and then along the top landing a further row of gold light-up balloons. Toddy spent ages staring up at the confetti-filled balloons, trying to work out how he could sabotage them at an appropriate time so that they exploded just as guests were making their way down the stairs, but finally had to give up as he decided that he could not carry out the dastardly deed in an anonymous manner!

The residents, regularly checking their watches and clocks, waited impatiently for the intervening hours to pass and for 8pm to arrive. It was agreed that each cat-eenager at Fremont House could invite a friend to join the party. Albert, wearing his interview suit and looking official, stood at the main door, checking each newcomer's credentials and entitlement to be there and double checking for anything that wasn't quite straightforward or that might be lurking in a pocket. Other than the confiscation of two jumping jack fireworks found in one deep pocket, all the visiting cat-eenagers were given the all-clear.

The last guest to arrive at the party was Hadden Hippo,

who was running late as it had taken him much longer than he expected to blow up all ten *Happy Supersonic Year Day* party balloons; he had been unable to hurry along the pavement with such an awkward jelly-like bundle to negotiate. There was much clapping and cheering as Hadden finally appeared at Fremont House and Albert and Burgatus rushed to help him manage his bouncing colourful consignment through the two main doors.

What a wonderful time they all had, dancing, singing, eating, and drinking. As darkness descended, the gathering moved up the several flights of stairs to the apartments on the two top floors, where the doors were all pushed wide open so that the city's scheduled firework spectacular could be viewed by all through the massive full-height picture windows. Generous plumes of dazzling multi-coloured extravaganza whizzed through the sky in dramatic and continuous bursts, triumphantly raining down from a great height over the River Rushmore. The Fremont House residents were silenced by the enormity and beauty of the spectacle and as the massive city bells clanked joyously, and with Toddy and Tilly squeakily accompanying the gathering on their bugles, they all joined together in many renditions of the traditional "Supersonic Year Day Ballad" with varying lyrics, as no one was quite sure of the right words.

Burgatus went downstairs ahead of the others and dimmed the lights in the reception area, and eventually, as the partygoers found their way back down, they shrieked with pleasure as the colourful mini sparklers on the elaborately iced honey fruit cake burst into life. Belltring, helped by Albert, cut and distributed large portions of the fruit cake that were neatly wrapped in colourful red and yellow flowered serviettes. They all toasted each other's future happiness and good health, with tall glasses full to overflowing with sweet strawberry wine for the seniors, and iced cordial for the juniors.

The residents unanimously agreed that they had never had such a memorable Supersonic Year Day party and the singing and cheering continued well into the early hours. Finally, to chants of encouragement, Burgatus Bulldog stood precariously on a chair to make his much awaited speech.

'What a wonderful time we have all had and next year we shall do it all over again. All that is needed is for everyone to contribute small regular donations to the tin in the reception area over the forthcoming months to pay for the eatables.'

At this remark the assembled gathering cheered and whistled so loudly that Burgatus struggled to make himself heard, but he went on, 'Deptus, Belltring Bulldog and I intend to finance the elaborately decorated celebration cake and the strawberry wine and cordial as a Honey Oak and Supersonic Year Day gift for all, not just for this year but for all future years to come!'

After this declaration, there were shrieks of delight and much clapping and stamping of paws.

Suddenly, and in a completely unplanned move, Burgatus lost his bearings on the chair and fell down flat on his face, taking the remains of the celebration cake with him. Fortunately, there were no injuries to report, just a rather sticky mess, and once Burgatus had been brushed down and tidied up the happy party came to its natural conclusion.

The young cat-eenager guests made their way outside to the waiting city vehicles scheduled to take them safely home, and the remaining residents of Fremont House slowly climbed the stairs to their beds.

Back at Windy Barn, it was just before midnight, and having eaten a hit-and-miss kind of an evening meal cooked by Bardwell, who had mistimed and muddled the various stages of the rather complicated menu, they all got suitably dressed against the chill night air and went out in the old Magatt to the beach, to watch the annual coastal firework display which as usual fell on Supersonic Year Day night.

They were just in time to see the dark cloudy sky illuminated by flares of glowing light which glided gently over the shimmering sea before slowly cascading down to form intricate multi-coloured patterns near the water's edge. A dynamic crescendo of explosions, whizzes, bangs, and pops followed as the cacophony competed with the sounds of the waves crashing onto the gravel shoreline; Daxham, transfixed by the whole event, found it almost impossible to calm down after their return to Windy Barn.

The next day Daxham suddenly became ill. At first Rilganna told him to "pull his socks up" which puzzled him as he wasn't wearing any socks. A little while later the poor penguin was unable to get himself up from his duvet; Rilganna called Peckleton and Bardwell to his bedside. They both looked anxiously at Daxham, who was feeling sick and looking listless, with his little flippers having turned an odd insipid colour, which was not a good sign.

Rilganna stayed near to Daxham all day long comforting him, keeping him cool and reading his favourite comic strips to him while Zig-Zag Pontoon remained watchful on a camp bed beside him. Hour by hour Daxham began to slowly perk up. It was only when Peckleton went to the store cupboard that he noticed a near-empty jar of pickled red cabbage. Daxham was unable to explain the phenomenon when quizzed about it, replying, 'I don't remember eating any of it.'

It was quite usual for Daxham to say that he didn't remember this or that when he wanted to avoid telling the truth. They were all relieved that the illness had been diagnosed. Daxham played on his discomfort for as long as he could until everyone's patience finally ran out, which coincided with their return to Waters-edge, with the annual celebrations over for another year.

14

More Activity at the Dental Clinic,
Birthday Dates and Challenging Behaviour

Six months had gone by and now the time had arrived for Rilganna to attend her next routine dental check-up at the clinic. To her astonishment she was once again referred by the junior partner to see Mr Scammondi Squirrel!

The same outcome as before transpired, with Mr Scammondi Squirrel confirming that another tooth needed to be replaced with the help of his new robotic dental device.

'It is the tooth next to one you have already had implanted that needs attention so my automatic magical robotic tooth implant machine is required once again to carry out the work, but this time the procedure will be a lot speedier, as I have become familiar with how the robot likes to work, and he knows me too,' said Mr Scammondi Squirrel, who was once again very keen to make Rilganna an appointment.

Rilganna felt reluctant about spending more funds on her teeth, but she was nevertheless persuaded by the others to go ahead and so the second robotic tooth replacement procedure was repeated the following week with a swiftness that surprised her. Mr Squirrel's charge had increased since the last procedure, which was rather a shock, as it was expensive enough the first time around.

When the job was completed, Mr Scammondi Squirrel showed Rilganna the newly implanted robotic tooth in the mirror as he had done on the first occasion, but this time it was at such a rapid turn of paw that she had been unable to see it clearly. She checked in her mouth with a mirror when she got home but wasn't able to identify the newly replaced tooth; however, putting her trust in Mr Scammondi Squirrel she was confident that she now had two magical automatic robotic teeth, and that all was well.

'Just before you go,' Mr Scammondi Squirrel had called out to Rilganna as she was about to leave the dental clinic, 'I have put a picture up on my large screen in the other consulting room for you to see, showing a third tooth in a poor state of repair so we had better book you in for that one to be replaced as well.'

Rilganna thanked him but, noticing that the tooth on the screen didn't look very much like one of hers, and feeling rather under pressure, she hurried away, promising to give the matter further thought; she was feeling confused and concerned and just wanted to get home.

Daxham had no idea when he had arrived in the world, and so about every four months or so he would claim a birthday, with the purpose of acquiring more gifts, especially from

Deptus who, being kind, regularly fell into the trap. The other residents of Waters-edge were becoming very embarrassed by his behaviour, so when Deptus arrived the following weekend, and with Daxham being elsewhere, they talked over the problem.

Rilganna started the discussion. 'I suggest that Daxham should have just one annual birthday, as that after all is a normal way of going on, and I suggest 30th June. If we schedule it, then there is more chance that the weather will be sunny and warm, and he can have his birthday tea outside, avoiding his sticky treats getting stuck all over the indoor floors.'

Rilganna was hoping that her suggestion would get unanimous approval from the others, and it did.

The wooden gavel, used to put finality to any important Waters-edge decision, was struck on the big kitchen table by Bardwell and the motion was carried there and then. Later that day Rilganna told Daxham about the new arrangement, which he took surprisingly well and even appeared to be pleased about!

Deptus arranged for an associate of his at Enterprise Wharf, who was a gifted and artistic calligrapher, to produce a professional-looking retrospective birth certificate for Daxham, who had it framed and fixed to his bedroom wall: it looked rather out of place, but anyway it was now all "official" and Daxham was content with the outcome, and it was one less problem for them to have to worry about.

Rilganna was also in need of an official birthday date, not because she kept claiming bogus birthdays like Daxham, but because she had no record of her beginning, as her birthday had never before been acknowledged. A long time ago she had made enquiries of the Ultorian Elderians, who had revealed nothing. In fact, the subject was greeted with detached indifference although she felt sure they knew the date but were not going to tell her when it was.

Rilganna was not keen to share a birthday date with Daxham, and the others quite understood the reasons why as it normally turned into a fiasco of some kind, so her birthday became registered on 31st July. It was unanimously decided that Zig-Zag Pontoon would also share Rilganna's birthday. Zig-Zag was not at all sure what it all meant but he was happy to join in anything that was going, especially as he was very keen on jigsaw puzzles and felt sure that someone would buy him a couple of new ones now that he had almost worn out his current stock: he had put his puzzles together so many times that he had managed to lose some of the crucial pieces. As gifts seemed to be the order of the day when anyone mentioned the word "birthday" he intended to drop a few hints.

Daxham's response to everyday occurrences was becoming erratic. It was making Rilganna, Bardwell, Peckleton and Zig-Zag feel uneasy. They were not able to foretell what he might do or say next, and they were becoming increasingly anxious. One particularly sunny Saturday morning brought about a notable example and brought the problem to a head. The colourful heads of the spring flowers were bobbing around in the light breeze outside Crindling's Community Hall, which was bedecked with brightly coloured bunting, it being the Annual Festival Weekend, a much-enjoyed village event looked forward to by residents young and old and those in between.

On the way back from the local shop on an errand for Rilganna, Daxham suddenly noticed that the Community Hall door was wide open, and he could hear the brass band tuning up their instruments, ready for the much-advertised charity concert. A queue was gathering in readiness for the entertainment to begin. Daxham made his way to the front of the queue to see what was going on as he had no concept of "waiting his turn", when he overheard a message-giver telling the main organiser that, due to the onset of a recurring health problem, the volunteer charged with collecting the entrance donations at the door would be unable to take up her post as promised.

'Oh dear,' said the organiser, muttering to himself and looking worried, 'what am I going to do now with no one to collect the entrance donations, and it's for charity, too.'

Daxham, hearing this and realising that the organiser was in a quandary just as the entertainment was shortly to begin, rapidly offered to help. He looked and sounded so genuine that the organiser agreed to his suggestion although at the back of his mind he somehow knew that this was probably a rash decision taken in the heat of the moment that would probably lead to trouble.

Daxham immediately took up his position by the main door and politely accepted the entrance donations. He was very pleased when he saw respectable sums being transferred from purses and pockets into the collection box. When everyone was seated and the concert began, Daxham put the collection box into his shopping bag and returned home.

After the concert was over, the organiser began searching here, there and everywhere for Daxham, who had completely vanished with the charity donations; feeling embarrassed, the organiser could not help wondering how and why his guard had been down and he had been so easily taken in.

Back at Waters-edge, it was about an hour later that Bardwell heard some tinkling of coins and upon investigation saw Daxham quietly counting out some money on his bed.

'Where did you get that box and money from?' asked Bardwell.

At this point Daxham explained how very kind the organiser had been in giving him a chance to collect charity collection donations at the Community Hall and that people had been very generous. Bardwell was lost for words and completely taken aback.

'Rilganna, come immediately,' shouted Bardwell, with panic in his voice.

'Oh dear,' said Rilganna, having listened to the tale of woe. 'What are we to do? This is a most distressing problem, and it must be sorted out without any delay. You are very stupid, Daxham, and this time I am very cross with you.'

Rilganna, who was normally patient with Daxham, in spite of the trouble that he often got into, was on this occasion exasperated, and as a result Daxham was badly shaken because of her unusual and unexpected reaction. She could hardly believe that Daxham, even though he had a knack of misconstruing things, could possibly have thought that the charity collection was meant for him, as some kind of gift. She put all the money back into the collection box and frogmarched Daxham back to the hall to talk to the organiser. En route Daxham was told exactly what he had to say, which was to include a sincere apology for the "confusion". He was to explain that he had only taken the box home to count out the money in the quiet of his room and here all the donations were, intact, and the whole thing had been a terrible misunderstanding, which of course it had been as far as Daxham was concerned.

They soon arrived at the hall and tracked down the distraught organiser which was not hard to do as he was being comforted by a sympathetic friend. After listening to Daxham's explanation the organiser was not at all convinced about its authenticity and looked at the bewildered penguin over his half-moon glasses with suspicion, and, it has to be said, with a hardening heart.

Daxham, sensing that this time he was in deep trouble and not really quite understanding why, started to make strange croaking sounds; after a short time grunts followed, and then, pausing only briefly to catch his breath, he started up again, with the decibels noticeably increasing with each new effort. In the end, the organiser, seeing the genuine distress and embarrassment that the situation was causing Rilganna, and being unable to stand the dreadful noise that Daxham was making, finally agreed to accept Daxham's apology and went along with Rilganna's suggestion that he should be added to the Community Hall's cleaning rota for the next six months to try and make up for the trouble he had caused.

Rilganna was cross and disappointed with Daxham for some days after this and he was told to do all the low dusting at Waters-edge for the foreseeable future, in order to take his turn fully trained when he joined the rota of the Community Hall's cleaning team.

The "misunderstanding" relating to the charity collection business continued to puzzle Daxham and his view remained the same; he considered the muddle not to have been his fault at all. As a consequence, he and the organiser continued to eye the other with suspicion, each being of a different opinion. Rilganna no longer wished to discuss the matter with Daxham and so it was never raised again.

Daxham enjoyed his period working at the Community Hall and carried out the dusting and cleaning in the lower reaches with enthusiasm and thoroughness, becoming quite a favourite with fellow dusters, who gave the little chap drinks, cakes and chocolate bars to keep him going, which was of course exactly what he wanted. He was ordered by Bardwell to donate two months' spending money to the Crindling Annual Festival's chosen charity, a concept which did not appeal to him one bit; on several occasions he tried to wriggle out of donating anything at all, but without success.

In spite of its protracted repercussions, Daxham learnt no lessons at all from the Community Hall debacle. Such an occurrence would have had a profound effect on a more sensitive individual but unfortunately the whole thing very quickly vanished from Daxham's thought processes and he soon forgot all about it. His behaviour continued to deteriorate and what's more he began to make inappropriate and insulting comments to anyone he found annoying.

***

It was the time of year when Matilda Chicken came along selling homemade biscuits and, as usual, she knocked at the door of Waters-edge. She baked these biscuits once a year to welcome the onset of spring (although no one knew quite why). Daxham considered the initiative to be a complete waste of time so, having opened the door, he told her to, "Chug off," and immediately banged the door shut again, in such haste that he knocked her basket of iced biscuits to the ground, also causing Matilda to catch the skirt of her dress in the door jamb which tore as she tried to free herself from her entrapment.

A terrible uproar ensued and, as a consequence, Bardwell felt obliged to buy all her damaged produce, but fortunately, as Rilganna was a skilled seamstress, an invisible repair was carried out to perfection on Matilda's damaged frock.

Rilganna told Daxham to buy Matilda the biggest box of chocolates he could find as well as offering an apology for his rudeness, both of which he did with bad grace and under duress. After this negative incident Matilda developed a morbid fear of baking and decided that she would never again produce her annual iced biscuits to welcome the spring, which, as it turned out, caused much unexpected local disappointment and she received many cards expressing sympathy for her unprovoked ordeal.

Another Waters-edge meeting was held as a significant decision had to be made, and with Deptus having come down for the weekend and Daxham tucked away watching one of his noisy DVDs, they got down to discussing the dilemma caused by Daxham's continuing bad behaviour.

Rilganna had been experiencing many restless nights puzzling over what could be done and then it suddenly occurred to her that the best solution was for Daxham to have an appointment with Ms Harriet Hare, a psychotherapist who lived locally. She had a reputation for being a firm but sympathetic practitioner with a good track record for achievement.

The problem had become urgent, as Daxham's carryings-on were causing trauma to the nervous and even some upset to others blessed with a more robust constitution. They unanimously agreed that Bardwell and Rilganna would call on Ms Hare the following week to explain their concern and to seek her advice with a view to obtaining a consultation for Daxham.

15

Mr Jeremiah Swan

When Jeremiah Swan relinquished his post as senior tea blender at a prominent firm of tea importers, having sold his fashionable Dunlace apartment at Swan Lodge, he chose not to seek out a neat country cottage, unlike so many of his contemporaries. Instead, Jeremiah decided to permanently rent a suite of rooms at the Swanningbell Mill Hotel at Crindling.

Jeremiah also decided to invest quite a bit of his savings in the Mill and was delighted when he was made an executive director at a special ceremony, an occasion that he was unlikely to ever forget such was its splendour; it was all the more remarkable coming quite unexpectedly as it did. His new responsibilities enabled him to remain useful and also safeguarded his residency in a permanent and secure way, which was reassuring at his time of life.

The beautiful Swanningbell Mill Hotel and Restaurant was just a little further along the river from Waters-edge and a more suitable location for a swan of Jeremiah's standing to rest his wings after many decades of hard and exacting work would have been almost impossible to find, and he knew that the wheel of good fortune had spun his way.

The Mill was a deliciously flamboyant castle-like building, delicately painted outside in soft greens, pinks and a gentle yellowy gold; its magnificence was further enhanced by sweeping diamond-shaped patterns rendered on its front walls. Juliet balconies in the traditional style supported window boxes extravagantly planted up, the results of which were voluptuous seasonal blooms lolling lazily over the ornate structures.

This ancient building willingly lent itself to luxurious hotel accommodation and attracted many discerning diners and those seeking a holiday of pleasure and relaxation. The grounds at the back of the old Mill were a delight. The snaking gravel paths with colourful flower beds either side enticed the garden-loving soul into a tranquil meditative rhythm of wanderings; age-old pond waters tumbled randomly and noisily over rocks and weirs, as they had done for centuries; hedges and trees received the care they deserved and the whole area was a joy to see at each season of the year, such was the skill of the head gardener and his two enthusiastic assistants.

Prior to settling his financial investment and taking up residence at the Swanningbell Mill Hotel, a thought came into Mr Swan's mind suggesting that he might try to find a partner with whom to share his autumn years; hitherto he had been too busy to invest the time needed in a serious-minded way.

Being well thought of in fashionable city circles, Jeremiah Swan not infrequently accepted invitations to elaborate dinner parties and saw these occasions as opportunities to meet new company, but sadly an amenable partner never materialised from these gatherings, although he did his utmost to appear both humorous and interesting to those he felt most inclined towards.

It was unfortunate but predictable that listeners became quickly uninterested in Jeremiah, whose topics of conversation were not appealing; he soon noticed when boredom was setting in (which had regularity about it). Having spent his whole working life being serious about the subject of tealeaf grading and its fluctuating market price, Jeremiah found it difficult to be frivolous and entertaining about a subject that he considered too important to be made light of. This was an awkward social impediment which led him to start rambling on in an unengaging way about absolutely anything that came into his head, pointless or not.

These unsuccessful social occasions would be followed by a period of misery, when he found his mind going over and over the evening's failings as he saw them, but there it was, he had done his best and so that was that.

One evening, nonchalantly navigating his computer with the help of his search engine, an advertisement popped up relating to the Goat & Rhino Internet Dating Agency, founded by Misses Goat and Rhino a few years earlier. The credentials of the agency appeared to be sound and respectable, and so he decided there and then to take out membership. He published photographs on the website (having posed well in careful rotation emphasising his best side) and then wrote an appropriate résumé about his life's achievements and his many personal attributes, as directed by the website coordinator. He considered that his overall "package" was pretty impressive. It was not too long before the agency made contact, having arranged for him to meet an eligible "swan" by the name of Geraldine.

At the arranged date and time Jeremiah arrived at the reception area of the smart Belvedere Restaurant in Landsmoth for the liaison and having tidied his feathers and straightened his tie he sat down on a comfortable chair and waited patiently. Geraldine, having seated herself in a similar chair opposite him, was also waiting good-naturedly for her suitor to arrive. Geraldine, it has to be said, looked elegant to a feather in a light blue soft velvet suit, a beautifully designed white cotton broderie anglaise blouse and smart black patent shoes. She was clutching a matching designer handbag that she had saved up for a long time to buy and as luck had it, patience and good timing had paid off, enabling her to make the purchase at sale time. She deserved this good fortune, as, generally speaking, Ms Geraldine Goose's life was not without its fair share of difficulties.

Although both were glancing at each other in an enquiring kind of way, it was a little while before the two realised their destiny.

'I hope you don't mind my asking,' said Mr Swan tentatively to Geraldine, who was in fact a goose, 'but I wonder whether you are here for the same purpose as I am and whether there has been some kind of mix-up. Are you awaiting a rendezvous organised by the Goat & Rhino Internet Dating Agency and perhaps you were expecting to meet a goose, as I was a swan?'

'Oh dear,' said Geraldine, blushing a little under her

feathers, 'I was thinking exactly the same, and yes, I am. I'm so sorry that I have turned out to be an unsuitable dinner guest.' Poor Geraldine, she had no need to apologise, and Jeremiah Swan told her so in a very positive way and what's more he felt annoyed that they, and particularly she, had been placed in this awkward situation by inefficiency, a failing which he had always had very little patience with. Jeremiah insisted that Geraldine must not get up to leave although she was all prepared to do so.

Mr Swan had nothing at all against geese and in fact two of his closest work colleagues had been geese, but things were not turning out in a way that he had imagined in his mind's eye when he took out his membership with the Goat & Rhino Internet Dating Agency and he was already becoming disillusioned by the whole process. It was hardly his fault that there were few eligible swans available in the vicinity, which was the excuse used by the agency's assistant to explain Geraldine's appearance when he queried it the next day.

However, the two would-be suitors, having met in these unexpected circumstances, were nonetheless content to dine together and soon the evening was going with a swing; jollity was in ready supply, helped along by glasses of exquisite dessert wine, a favoured delicacy that they both shared.

'I had an unfortunate experience via this same dating agency a couple of weeks ago,' said Geraldine during her dinner conversations with Jeremiah. 'It turned out that due to an error on the agency's computer I was partnered with a most unappealing eagle. He was a very precise and terse individual, and much bad feeling was dramatically played out in the public arena, as we met in the reception area of the stylish Picardo Hotel and Restaurant.

'Upon seeing me he was greatly disappointed: he flapped his huge wings, knocking over several bottles and wine glasses that were perched on small tables nearby. He caused a most terrible scene, squawking and complaining of his precious time having been wasted and in the end security personnel were summoned to escort him from the premises and I was sent home in a taxi. I was so embarrassed that I went straight to bed, pulling the duvet tightly over my head, and I remained there for two days before I had the courage to get up again.'

Mr Swan tried hard to keep his good manners up to scratch and to look serious, but he thought this story was hugely funny; it appealed to his sense of humour, and in the end, he was unable to suppress the huge gusts of laughter which eventually shot out through his beak at an enormous turn of speed like a tornado through a tunnel. The hilarity was so infectious that Geraldine soon joined in, and they became exhausted by merriment. As a consequence their friendship was firmly cemented.

It was the first time that Geraldine had been able to see the funny side of the ill-fated blind date with the eagle, the memory of which had caused her to feel hot and bothered under her wings every time she thought about it, which was frequently, but now having told Jeremiah Swan the story she felt liberated, lifted up and so much more cheerful than before, and soon the miserable memory began to melt away.

After Jeremiah's dinner date with Geraldine, silence emanated from the dating agency and then after a delay of several weeks the agency contacted him again. This time they had arranged for him to liaise with an eligible swan who, they said, lived some twenty miles northwards. Mr

Swan was dubious; after all, as he reminded himself at the time, he had already experienced an inefficiently organised assignation, courtesy of the internet dating agency, when he first met Geraldine, although he did not look back on this arrangement with any regret as it turned out to be a most pleasant experience and was the foundation of a new and fulfilling friendship for them both.

With the agency's assurance that on this occasion he was definitely to meet a swan, Jeremiah took the initiative and caught a train north to Doodleton on the next available Saturday morning and made contact with Sophie Quipp via their mobile phones during the outward journey. During their conversation Jeremiah found her to be friendly and enthusiastic and so it was arranged that they would meet that very evening.

Sophie Quipp had decided in advance where she wanted to go and so it was that they met at the door of the Thueris Club in Doodleton town centre at 9pm. Jeremiah was a little taken aback when he first saw Sophie Quipp in person, as she was wearing a luminous sparkling pink outfit covered in loosely stitched sequins, the fashion of which he had never seen before, and what's more, her feathers were dyed an unusual gingery-orangey colour.

Jeremiah was immediately dubious about her choice of venue as it looked a bit on the seedy side (not his cup of tea at all). A giant-sized bouncer positioned at the entrance was looking him up and down in a frosty kind of way and Jeremiah was already feeling out of his comfort zone before ever he got inside the premises. He was already wishing that he had stayed home but unfortunately the scene was set whether he liked it or not and he could see no way of escape.

The entrance fee to the premises was substantial, especially when doubled up, and Jeremiah embarrassed himself by waiting for some change to come from the note that he had given the doorman; but none was forthcoming, although he continued to ponder awkwardly for quite some time in hopeful anticipation.

Once inside the club Sophie was bewitched by the heady atmosphere. She appeared to forget that she was Jeremiah's guest. She immediately propelled herself onto the crowded wooden dance floor and began enthusiastically doing a kind of hip-hop rotating jive. The sequinned skirt on her skimpy dress was flying through the air, like a hot air balloon in flight, as she partnered a variety of eligible clubbers, but not Jeremiah, which was just as well as the atmosphere was far too hot and noisy for him.

The psychedelic flashing lights were making him feel a little funny in the head and unsteady on his legs and he wished he had brought his sunglasses with him to protect his eyes, which soon had funny little moving blobs in front of them. The light-headedness he was experiencing was not helped by crowds of people knocking into him; what's more, a few of the revellers were shouting things at him which he was unable to hear above the rising beat of the pulsating music. Togged out in his usual elegant and refined style, he felt inappropriately dressed in his best lounge suit, dark blue patent shoes, white shirt, and blue spotted bow tie. In addition to which, tiredness was catching up with him after the tedious train journey; how he wished that the floor would just swallow him up so that he could vanish from sight.

All in all, the night out cost Jeremiah Swan quite a hefty sum as he seemed to be buying extortionately priced alcoholic refreshments and expensive snacks right, left and centre for all kinds of oddly dressed strangers, which apparently accounted for the very large bill he was presented with as he was about to leave. At the end of this rather trying evening, Sophie Quipp told Jeremiah that she didn't think they were at all suited and as a consequence she had no desire to meet with him again. Although he felt exactly the same way about her, Jeremiah returned home feeling bewildered and emotionally drained by the whole disappointing experience. After all, he did have some feelings, and so he decided there and then to cancel his membership with the dating agency and to give up the idea of finding a partner, instead choosing to move to Crindling to reside permanently in comfortable surroundings at the Swanningbell Mill Hotel.

Thankfully things worked out happily for Mr Swan and any unhappy experiences he had encountered soon faded into oblivion. He was much appreciated and respected at the Mill and all kinds of good things arose for him to enjoy. He bought himself a second-hand river-worthy craft which he saw advertised in the local post office window; he moored it at the side of the old mill pond. In addition, he enjoyed private swimming facilities as no one else seemed to use them, and above all he enjoyed comfortable accommodation and good company right on his doorstep, so life in general was very interesting for him and often quite amusing. From then on, he settled down to his new lifestyle in an independent, contented kind of way, enjoying the simple pursuits and pleasures of the locality.

From his permanent table in the dining room positioned at one of the spacious bay windows overlooking the tranquil gardens, Jeremiah could enjoy all his meals, sometimes entertaining those lucky enough to receive one of his much sought-after invitations.

Jeremiah Swan was frequently irritated by Daxham. He considered him to be a thoughtless and stupid individual and he had no time for him. Daxham often referred to Mr Swan as "Swanny" which annoyed him intensely, especially when he shouted out loudly, 'Morning Swanny!' as he so often did whatever the time of day. Jeremiah found that ignoring him did not bring about the desired effect, and Daxham continued to be irksome.

Sometimes Jeremiah would invite Deptus, Peckleton, Bardwell and Zig-Zag Pontoon for evening drinks and snacks (Zig-Zag didn't eat anything, of course, but loved the company). On other occasions he would ask Rilganna to join him for afternoon tea and cake, especially when Geraldine was staying as Mr Swan's guest at the Swanningbell Mill. Mr Swan never invited Daxham for any social interaction although the little penguin waited patiently and, when an invitation card came through the door, he hastened to the letterbox, hoping that this time it would be his turn.

Daxham was disheartened by this omission and although he appeared to be insensitive to the disappointment the opposite was in fact true, and he hated being left out. One summer's afternoon Daxham confided in Deptus, who was swinging back and forth in his hammock between the willow and the old apple tree, and asked him, 'Why do you think I never get an invitation to spend time with Mr Swan, Deptus?'

Deptus didn't know what to answer, and as he didn't want to hurt Daxham's feelings he pretended that he had fallen asleep in the sun. In actual fact, Deptus didn't really know why Daxham was left out of invitations received from

Jeremiah Swan because he was unaware that he called him "Swanny"; he just assumed that Daxham's dubious reputation had gone before him, which in a sense it had.

It was in the late autumn, during an evening spent with Jeremiah, that Deptus took the opportunity of bringing the subject of Daxham's disappointment to his host's attention but Jeremiah made it quite clear that he had no intention of reversing his opinion of "that stupid penguin" which was very poor and therefore no invitation was likely to be forthcoming, now or in the future, and the discussion was swiftly brought to a close without further embellishment.

Fate, though, took a hand as, some weeks later, on a particularly frosty winter's night, Daxham was wandering around the perimeter of the Swanningbell Mill near the car park to see whether there was anything interesting going on when he saw two undesirables scratching away at Jeremiah's smart new red sports car with a key. Daxham could, of course, have walked on by, but he didn't. Challenging the two scallywags with all the robustness that he could muster for his small size all he got for his good deed was a biff across the head; the little chap was knocked to the ground and roughly shoved and pushed around.

Just as all this unpleasantness was going on two guests leaving the hotel saw what was happening and ran to Daxham's aid. He was returned home in a state of shock and disarray with his new winter trousers ruined by splits and tears that couldn't be patched.

The next day all these happenings were fed back to Jeremiah Swan, who was completely taken aback to hear of Daxham's bravery. As it turned out, Daxham was included in the next social evening that Mr Swan held at the Mill and was particularly thanked there and then for his exemplary action. Daxham wore his newish brown trousers and yellow shirt for the occasion and was on his very best and politest behaviour which could be okay-ish when he put his mind to it.

Just as he was leaving to go home, Jeremiah handed Daxham an envelope: it turned out to be a note of thanks handwritten on Jeremiah's expensively embossed headed notepaper, along with a generous voucher to be spent at the local outfitters on a new pair of good quality winter trousers and a matching winter cap. For once Rilganna was proud of Daxham and he had quite a few treats as a result, but she not infrequently reminded him that he must never ever again call Mr Swan "Swanny", and he never did.

16

*Psychotherapy, More Bad Behaviour
and Comfortable Paws*

Bardwell and Rilganna's initial visit to Ms Hare's consulting rooms (situated above Sprocket's greengrocer's shop in the middle of Crindling by the bus station) to discuss Daxham's behaviour and to ask whether she would be willing to see Daxham for a consultation had been successful.

They explained to the psychotherapist how his general demeanour had deteriorated and how insulting he was to others when interacting with them, especially if he found a particular individual annoying. Ms Hare was confident that she could help although the case did sound rather challenging.

As Bardwell was speaking to Ms Harriet Hare, he found her penetrating gaze a little disarming; it was as though she could see inside his mind. On the other hand, Bardwell thought if she was able to see into the depths of Daxham's mind that could be a great asset, as no one at Waters-edge had ever managed it.

The following Friday, wearing his second-best brown suit, Daxham was accompanied by Rilganna and Bardwell to attend the first of his appointments. Daxham, it had to be said, was a most reluctant client. He looked very miserable as he walked along the lane between them, slowly dragging himself towards the "dreaded destination": he just couldn't understand why he had to bother with such "utter nonsense" and would have dumped the whole shebang and absconded, if only he thought that he could have got away with it.

When they arrived at Ms Hare's rooms there was a short wait before the psychotherapist appeared. Having introduced herself, Ms Hare gently welcomed Daxham to the practice and in doing so her manner almost bordered on the apologetic. He then went off with her for the start of his consultation in the inner room with the door shut. Rilganna and Bardwell sat quietly if not a little nervously in the waiting area just outside.

There was calm for the first ten minutes and then suddenly a loud high-pitched screech was heard, and the consulting room door flew wide open. Daxham exploded through the door as indelicate language tumbled out through his beak; tears of temper were falling rhythmically downwards, eventually arriving as a light shower on the surface of his jumper, peppering it with moisture and making a spotty mess.

Rilganna, leaving Daxham with Bardwell, tip-pawed cautiously into the consulting room where she found Ms Harriet Hare in a rattled state, which was not surprising having just been at the receiving end of one of Daxham's "difficult turns". Her head was resting limply on the table while the rest of her was twitching in an agitated way. Rilganna hurried away to fetch her a glass of cold water and opened the window in the hope of reviving her with an abundance of fresh air, but Ms Hare remained the same for some little while, until gradually she began to regain her composure.

'Never in my whole professional career,' Ms Hare remarked, as Rilganna, now accompanied by Bardwell, continued to stare at her with an anxious expression, 'have I ever felt so out of my comfort zone in a clinical situation, having to deal with such an impudent and out of control client who is so reluctant to be helped.'

As they got ready to leave her consulting rooms Bardwell remarked, 'I really am very sorry to have brought this trouble upon you, Ms Hare.'

He was truly troubled by her shocked expression and with sincerity in his voice he went on, 'I do so hope that a good night's sleep will set the problem straight.'

With this final comment having been made, the three of them returned to Waters-edge in silence. Daxham was already looking a good bit more cheerful, having escaped from Ms Harriet Hare and her irritating, searching questions.

Daxham continued with his antisocial behaviour, having conveniently chosen to forget the consultation experience with Ms Hare as though it had never taken place: Daxham always found it easy to erase unpleasant memories from his mind, and he certainly didn't want any repeat visits. He was very hopeful that he "had seen her off" and was fairly confident that, after the first encounter, she would avoid any further appointments to see him if Bardwell or Rilganna were to approach her again.

A couple of weeks later Rilganna finally plucked up enough courage to contact Ms Hare again, hoping that she might be prepared to see Daxham for a second time. The psychotherapist didn't show a lot of enthusiasm when the request was made, but in the end, she reluctantly agreed to embark on a further session, although in truth she wished the challenge hadn't come her way again. She felt very annoyed with herself afterwards, that she had not been quick-witted enough to think of a good excuse to avoid any further contact with Daxham but unfortunately, she had been surprised by the phone call and caught off-guard, which had rendered her mentally unarmed.

In truth, Ms Hare was not at all satisfied with how she had dealt with Daxham at his initial appointment as she put a very high standard on all that she did. She would have been more content had she been able to control the situation in a more professional way, and as a consequence, she became concerned that her reputation might be at risk, having got involved with such an uncooperative and annoying client.

In her spare time, as a result of this insecurity, she had been studying some unusual case histories in the literature in preparation for any repeat consultations, should "misfortune" bring Daxham back to her consulting rooms again; and so sorting out this rather tricky case was now a matter of professional pride for Ms Hare, and she felt obliged to press on. She knew that she had to avoid getting discombobulated by Daxham's erratic behaviour and that this called for strong mental discipline that she now felt better prepared for. She had dug herself into a hole; she wished fate had not dealt her an unenviable challenge but now the situation had to be dealt with as best it could.

At the second appointment things settled down in a more peaceful way. This was mainly because Daxham, having sat up very late watching an action-packed wild-west film, was finding Harriet Hare's couch rather comfortable.

Ms Hare, staring penetratingly at Daxham, said in a secretive whisper, 'Now tell me all about your past life before the commencement of your new existence at Waters-edge; don't spare any details, however incriminating you might think they sound, as I shan't be judging you in any negative way.'

Daxham went very quiet as he struggled to think of what to say, as in truth he had absolutely no intention of discussing any such thing. Just as Daxham was beginning to feel trapped by desperation, another client unexpectedly appeared at the reception desk and Ms Hare was called away to attend to a matter of great urgency that needed her instant attention.

During her absence Daxham slowly drifted off to sleep. Upon her return Ms Hare found her client to be in such a drowsy state that she was unable to stir him. His intellectual alertness (such as it ever was) had all but gone and by the time she had succeeded in brightening him up the appointment was out of time and again no progress to speak of was made. Bardwell sighed but he and Rilganna had to remain hopeful, there being no other option.

**

Daxham's old boat that he had arrived in all that time ago was swiftly disposed of shortly after his arrival, as it was unsafe and an eyesore, stuck as it was at the bottom of the garden.

A new craft was purchased in its place for all at Waters-edge to enjoy. It was a simple rowing boat that had been fitted with seats which were upholstered in a striking shade of lime green. For additional comfort there was also a collection of soft loose cushions covered in a gold star pattern, and thick blankets for chillier days were stored at the stern. The boat was kept on the riverbank and protected with a waterproof cover to shield it from inclement weather.

One Saturday the boat was settled in the water as Peckleton had already enjoyed a quiet meander along the river in the early morning sun, soaking up the peaceful tranquillity of the new day. Later that morning, Daxham, wandering down the garden, saw the boat resting in the river and thought he might take himself off for a row, and so he climbed into *Maisie* and drifted off towards the Swanningbell Mill Hotel to see what news there was about.

As he rowed closer to the millpond, he noticed a smart wedding reception in full flight in the flower-bedecked grounds of the hotel. Refreshments were clearly visible, champagne corks were popping and the enticing liquid was flowing freely. He could see the beautiful bride, the centre of attention, looking magnificent in her white organza gown with its long, elegant train. Daxham, glancing down, noticed that he was wearing a respectable pair of trousers and an equally decent jacket and so he quietly tied *Maisie* up at the Mill's landing dock, and hurriedly made his way towards the collected gathering.

'I'll go and see what's going on. I'm pretty sure that attending this smart occasion could be a good tactical move for me. In addition to which there might be something worthwhile for me to enjoy and I have nothing important in my diary for today,' said Daxham, thinking out loud. Not that

Daxham ever had any pressing commitments that he placed the slightest importance on, whether they were written in his diary or not.

He soon made himself at home at the wedding party and sampled all that there was available. Seeing that the commencement of the wedding breakfast was shortly to be announced and spotting an opportunity, he hastened into the dining hall, turned one of the name cards over and wrote *Master Daxham P* on the reverse side. As the guests assembled for the meal, an invitee was looking a bit lost as he was unable to find his name card at the table. This caused some inconvenience and embarrassment as the unfortunate guest had to be squeezed in at the far end, away from those he should have been seated with.

This did not put the management in a very good light and there was a lot of apologising to the displaced individual for the unexpected irritation and some puzzlement as to how this muddle could possibly have happened. It was not very pleasant to hear members of staff squabbling and blaming each other for the anomaly and the dispute went on for some considerable time, but Daxham was very good at detaching himself from any trouble that emanated from his behaviour, and he cheerfully chipped in with all the background grumbling that was going on.

'How very inefficient,' Daxham blurted out in his most refined voice to a nearby guest, who, without hesitation, enthusiastically agreed. Encouraged by this acknowledgment, Daxham went on, 'You would think that an upmarket establishment such as this would have ensured that all the guests' name cards were sorted and placed efficiently around the table, wouldn't you!'

Fellow guests, not wishing to pursue the "complaining" any longer, in case it started to endanger the serenity of the occasion, were beginning to put space between themselves and Daxham, not that he took any notice of that.

At this most elegant of occasions Daxham declared to all and sundry how he was well connected in various ways to the main participants, telling some that he was an established family friend, and others that he was a close personal friend of the bride, or similarly of the groom. During the duration of the second course Daxham started hiccoughing and it was not long before he drifted off to sleep, having hastily drunk too much champagne in the absence of his favourite ginger beer. He then began to snore in a raucous way, as was his fashion, and finally he slipped off his chair and ended up under the table, such that he had to be pulled out and removed by the two fellow guests sitting either side of him. For some minutes after Daxham's retrieval, the remaining guests in the nearby seats were trying to work out among themselves who had actually known the mystery guest, and gave up when they came to no satisfactory conclusion.

In Daxham's pocket an address was found by his rescuers in a rather scruffy old notebook and Daxham was delivered back home in an unsightly heap, still snoring, to a most embarrassed Bardwell who put him straight to bed. Meanwhile *Maisie* had to remain where she was until the following morning when Peckleton went discreetly along to rescue her and bring her back to her Waters-edge mooring. Fortunately, Jeremiah Swan was away holidaying in Otland and by the time he returned this particular very awkward incident had been forgotten.

Daxham continued to have consultations with Ms Hare and all in all it took five sessions before there was any noticeable change in his behaviour. He gradually became less selfish and rude in his day-to-day interactions with others. Sometimes, though, he would start to say something contentious or offensive but a look from Rilganna or Bardwell, always alert to any possible infringements, normally curtailed his thought process. Ms Hare was of the opinion that being congratulated by Jeremiah Swan at the time of the sports car incident had boosted his self-confidence, and the recent noticeable improvement in his behaviour was partly due to a delayed reaction to this positive event which had helped towards the progress he had since made.

An arrangement was left with the psychotherapist that Bardwell and Rilganna would bring Daxham for a routine appointment every six months, unless there was an emergency, and that way she would be able to keep a check on him for any noticeable signs of deterioration.

Ms Harriet Hare continued to be very much engaged in studying her textbooks and for much of the time she seemed preoccupied. A distracted expression had taken over her normally serene appearance and those who knew her well saw a transformation in her behaviour that was out of character. Daxham was rather apt to change the lives of others once they got involved with him, and some became unsure of themselves for some time afterwards, but, barring a few rare exceptions, most regained their equilibrium in the end.

It had taken patience and persistence but at long last Deptus managed to persuade Peckleton to do less jogging and more gardening, citing wear and tear on his knees. This was partly out of a genuine concern for Peckleton's wellbeing but also because when Deptus stayed at Waters-edge he found himself being asked by Peckleton to sit outside on a fishing stool to time him on his runs, as he jogged along on a continuous path around the lanes. This was not too bad in the summer as Deptus just about managed to keep awake reading his book in the sun while occasionally looking at the stopwatch and putting the times and speeds accomplished by Peckleton into his notebook. In the depths of the winter though this was far from a pleasant experience as Deptus found himself almost frozen to the spot: it was too cold for him to nod off and the endurance was causing the development of chilblains which led to itchy discomfort and pain on his paws, in spite of his wearing his cosy woolly socks and thick-soled cold weather boots.

Deptus knew that Peckleton would need a substantial project to take the place of his regular jogging routine as he liked to be busy all the time, and finally he thought of an idea. He suggested to Peckleton that he set up a stall at the front of Waters-edge to sell the surplus vegetables, fruit and flowers that he grew in the garden. Peckleton was immediately taken up with the idea, and Rilganna, hearing about this, was so keen that she went out and bought a large set of scales and became in charge of weighing, pricing and bagging up the goods. Bardwell, too, was in favour of the new venture as it brought in extra funds, some of which could be spent on Windy Barn, which always needed a job or six doing.

Deptus was relieved that his suggestion turned out to be popular, and more so that his paws were spared. The enterprise was a great success, gradually growing in complexity. In the summer Rilganna began to produce sandwiches, using their fresh seasonal salad and crunchy carrots, which were more popular than they could ever have imagined, with the lunch-time queues outside Waters-edge growing ever longer by the day. Zig-Zag Pontoon was kept busy making loaves of bread in a bread-making machine bought for the new enterprise and ensuring that the shelves were fully stocked up for the customers.

Hibberley Heron was always first in the lunch-time queue, as he found the sandwiches delicious and substantial, and it saved him a job in the morning, enabling him to get an earlier start on his window cleaning responsibilities as a result. Rilganna made sure that he had an extra-thick slice of fruit cake in his sandwich bag each day, as Hibberley continued to look a little peaky with such a heavy workload to contend with.

17

Those Teeth Again, and a Fresh Challenge

Since seeing the picture of that "third" tooth on Mr Scammondi Squirrel's screen at the end of her last appointment at the dental clinic, Rilganna continued to ponder on the reported poor condition of her teeth as she really had no idea that they were in such bad shape, but were they?

She was still doubtful whether that "third" tooth, shown to her by Mr Squirrel on his large screen, was actually one of hers. The whole experience had a shadowy aspect to it and was rather playing on her mind.

As it turned out, the saga relating to the tooth scenario continued for Rilganna in an unexpected way, for recently she had noticed that a curious sensation had developed around the area of one of her two new robotic teeth, and something did not feel at all right.

Rilganna made an appointment to see Mr Scammondi Squirrel the following day. He was keen to talk to her at first and hastened to greet her, as he was under the impression that she was going ahead with the fitting of a third robotic replacement tooth. This was not the case, of course, much to Mr Scammondi Squirrel's intense disappointment, which was plain to see, and as Rilganna began to explain her worries to the dentist his increasingly impatient attitude was beginning to cause waves of discontentment to permeate the room.

'I am experiencing a most peculiar sensation around the area of my two new automatic magical robotic teeth that you and the tooth robot recently fitted me up with, and I would like to know which one of the two is causing the problem. I am hoping that you can solve the mystery for me and put it right,' said Rilganna, trying not to be too distracted by the now very unpleasant atmosphere that had arisen between herself and Mr Scammondi Squirrel, who puffed out his chest, gritted his teeth together and began to look openly irritable.

Rilganna was taken aback to see this side of his personality which was quite different to how he normally was.

'I have never heard of such a thing,' retorted Mr Squirrel in his sharply worded reply. 'In any case, you have only ever had one new magical robotic tooth implanted at my dental clinic, not two. The mysterious sensation you speak of is nothing whatsoever to do with me and I have no wish to pursue this matter any further as I am very busy today, tomorrow and for many days to come.'

Rilganna was astonished and completely taken aback. She could see that Mr Scammondi Squirrel was adamant and rigid in his declaration and that no further discussion on the subject was about to take place.

When Rilganna had regained a little more composure, she took a deep breath and continued to enquire further.

'Then what was that second payment for, if it was not for the installation of a second magical robotic tooth? I suggest, Mr Scammondi Squirrel, that you should consult your records detailing my past appointments and treatment.'

Rilganna waited for a reaction, but Mr Squirrel made no clear reply, in fact, he made no reply at all. He wasn't at all interested in anything Rilganna had to say, but still she went on, 'In my opinion, Mr Squirrel, you are a disgrace to your profession, and I am very disappointed in the way that you have dealt with my dental problem. In fact, you have not even tried to put my mind at rest or to sort out my discomfort. I am now beginning to think that you used your newfangled machine on the first occasion to replace a tooth which could easily have been treated in a more conventional way. To be sure one of these days you will get your comeuppance because fraudsters and tricksters usually do in the end!'

Rilganna was shaking with fury, but Mr Squirrel ignored the presence of his agitated patient and as it became obvious that she was being frozen out in the manner of the ice age, she eventually felt obliged to leave the clinic.

On her way home Rilganna's mind was in a state of disbelief, it had been such an unpleasant experience, but then, all of a sudden, a jolt of realisation rapidly sped through Rilganna's head like an electric shock; it caused her head to spin, so much so that she almost tumbled over. It must have been that Mr Squirrel had pretended that the robot had implanted another tooth on her second visit to the dental clinic, which is why the procedure had been so fast and why he had told her that the technique had speeded up now that he and the tooth robot had become more familiar! This bogus tooth procedure was carried out for no good reason other than for Mr Scammondi Squirrel to obtain more money from her: there was in fact no "second" magical replacement robotic tooth; it didn't exist.

Rilganna was in a daze when she arrived back at Waters-edge. She hurried straight upstairs and sat quietly staring into her mouth with a mirror, feeling somewhat taken aback, for on close scrutiny she could now see that in fact she only had one new robotic tooth because she identified a tiny pulsating robotic glow on the top of that one tooth. She searched very carefully but there was no evidence of a second robotic glow anywhere else in her mouth.

If only she had been diligent, and had checked more carefully after that second visit, she would have noticed the absence of a second new robotic tooth, but instead she had taken Mr Scammondi Squirrel's word on trust and had never dreamt of such a deception, and so it was that poor Rilganna continued to agonise and ponder. This preoccupation led to introspection and for a while she became intensely self-analytical and suffered a kind of identity crisis. Why had she been singled out and made a fool of in such an obvious way; was it that she appeared unworldly or just plain stupid?

In the end she grew exhausted by her deliberations; she was getting no peace of mind and she felt worn down, so she decided there and then that she must try to let the matter drop out of her thoughts, move on and balance her mind.

As a result of Daxham's more mature behaviour which had been gradually evolving since his therapy sessions with Ms Hare, Deptus thought up a challenge for him, and to his great surprise he got a good response. He persuaded Daxham to advertise himself as a "personal shopping helper" offering a service to those locally requiring individual attention. Astonishingly he soon attracted some interested clients and before long he had quite a respectable list of orders each week as he turned out to be reliable and efficient, if not a little over-eager.

His eagerness stemmed from his inability to pass by a bargain, and it caused a weak link in the system. He would sometimes come back with purchases which were not on the shopping list for the client that he was dealing with, just because they happened to be "on offer", but he didn't think about the appropriateness of the items concerned and it led to complications.

It was completely pointless buying two boxes of bargain dishwasher tablets for Wilfred Dormouse, who, living alone, made very little washing up and he certainly didn't have any sophisticated mechanical devices in his small home. Then there was the purchase of a multi-pack of tinned sweetcorn that Daxham bought with Ms Rosalinda Redshank in mind. She only normally ate shellfish so that was just another example of a pointless purchase.

It was on these occasions that he had to be helped out of a scrape, and Rilganna was left feeling obliged to pay for miscellaneous items that she didn't want or need, but it was a price worth paying to keep Daxham busy and useful, and she felt she had to support the new venture if that was what it took. She felt it was counterproductive to get angry with him, as for once he was trying to be useful, although inadvertently he ended up causing problems, as he always did one way or another.

18

*An Unexpected Inheritance and
Peckleton Gets to the Bottom of Things*

An official-looking airmail letter arrived via the post
person. It had a Nimblewissian postmark addressed to
Mr H B L Badger. It was firmly stamped "Personal", which
made it all the more intriguing. Daxham, who always
collected the post as soon as it was pushed through the
letterbox, ran to Bardwell with the letter. Bardwell looked
at it with a puzzled expression and placed it to one side. By
this time Rilganna, Peckleton and Zig-Zag Pontoon had all
joined Daxham in gathering around Bardwell, unable to
keep their curiosity under control.

Bardwell, unable to quell the interest that his letter had
generated, was reluctantly pushed into opening the envelope.
His astonishment grew as he read out loud the following oddly
worded communication from a firm of lawyers situated in an

area of deepest and wildest Nimblewissia called Pelliwig. It began:

Dear Mr Hinderlay Bardwell Lucifer Badger,

We are writing to you regarding an important matter relating to a family legacy and we are thus instructed by our client, being your first cousin, once removed, Mr Catherton Badger, to clarify a certain position. As you will probably recall Mr Catherton Badger is the only offspring of your first cousin, Mr Firbank Badger.

Some time ago your great-uncle Mr Branchwood Badger of Pelliwig (your deceased father's uncle) sadly died having lived to an extraordinarily respectable age, and in his will he left a large tract of forest land in the area of the Mighty Wooded Badger Plateau to Mr Catherton Badger, who had in fact already taken on the complete estate management of the forest on behalf of Mr Branchwood Badger, then in his dotage, who, being unable to cope with the responsibility for some time, was very glad to have this help. However, a smaller, separate tract of land and forest was left by the deceased, Mr Branchwood Badger, to a certain Mr Hinderlay Bardwell Lucifer Badger.

It is a matter of great concern to Mr Catherton Badger that his first cousin, once removed, Mr Hinderlay Bardwell Lucifer Badger, had not been able to make claim to this part of the estate, rightfully his own, as it turned out to be difficult to track down the location of the aforementioned Mr Hinderlay Bardwell Lucifer Badger.

Mr Catherton Badger has spent much time and expense seeking the whereabouts of Mr Hinderlay Bardwell Lucifer Badger and now at long last he hopes, having engaged this firm's assistance, to have tracked you down as being the correct Mr Hinderlay Bardwell Lucifer Badger, so to speak. I may mention that during the intervening period, Mr Catherton Badger has also been estate managing the aforementioned additional tract of land in the manner of his own, in order to keep everything in order. This has been done without hesitation and with the kindest of intentions.

If you are able to confirm that you are the correct Mr Hinderlay Bardwell Lucifer Badger, and can prove your relationship to Messrs Branchwood Badger (unfortunately, the late) and Catherton Badger (still very much in the present), the land is to be officially handed over to you in adherence to the strict Laws of our Land. The exact size of the tract of forest involved in the legacy will be revealed to you in detail in due course, once the title of ownership has been settled.

I await your swift reply and further instructions which will be dealt with in the manner of our usual efficiency.

Meanwhile I remain your obedient servant in all the most lawful of respects,

Yours as ever, and without a doubt always most sincerely,

Signed: Percy P Podworthy of Podworthy and Partners of Pelliwig in Rural Nimblewissia.

Bardwell felt exhausted after reading out the rather peculiar and elongated letter and paused for a little to catch his breath. For a time they all stood in complete silence staring at Bardwell, in part because it was new to them that he had such an impressive set of names. Daxham managed to keep quiet although he thought it was very funny and was finding it a struggle to swallow a giggle that was gurgling up in his beak. Rilganna was the first to speak.

'Are Mr Catherton Badger and Mr Branchwood Badger, as mentioned in the letter, two of your relatives, Bardwell; has the law firm found the right Mr Hinderlay Bardwell Lucifer Badger?'

'I am aware of a Great-Uncle Branchwood Badger, but I know very little about him, so he is in effect only a name to me,' replied Bardwell, looking glum.

Bardwell was unable to deny that he was the correct Hinderlay Bardwell Lucifer Badger although in his heart of hearts he dearly wished he could have said otherwise.

By now Daxham was quite overcome with excitement, as he could see shooting the rapids in the wilds of Nimblewissia to be the start of an exciting new way of life, full of opportunity and zing. He was looking forward to having a large purpose-built Pelliwig home erected in the Mighty Wooded Badger Plateau with no luxury spared. Rilganna, Peckleton and Zig-Zag Pontoon ignored Daxham and his effervescent behaviour as they felt greatly for Bardwell, who was beginning to look a little faint with the shock. How he wished that the letter had got lost in the post; but it hadn't, and the matter needed to be dealt with. They all agreed that they would seek Deptus' advice when he came down to see them at the weekend, and so Bardwell tucked the letter back into its envelope for the time being and tried hard to put the bothersome issue out of his mind.

Recently, all at Waters-edge had noticed that Rilganna had become quiet and subdued, spending more time alone and deep in thought. She wasn't even interested in telling Daxham off when he was being irritating, which he found rather disconcerting, because he liked Rilganna's attention even though this often meant that he was in her bad books.

Peckleton decided that he must get to the bottom of the mystery and find out what was wrong. When they had finished their breakfast that Wednesday morning and with everyone else having gone their separate ways, Peckleton sat down next to Rilganna at the kitchen table and, talking with her firstly about general matters, he gradually found out about the strange saga of the missing magical robotic tooth. Peckleton was puzzled when he heard the revelation and not a little shocked, as he had never heard such a strange story about a tooth before. He felt sympathy for Rilganna and tried to soothe her troubled mind.

Later that evening Peckleton sat with Bardwell in his office and, diverting him from his work, told him the story that Rilganna had told him earlier that morning.

'Well, I never did!' said Bardwell. 'What a miserable event for poor Rilganna to have experienced but she must not trouble herself about it, and I shall tell her so.'

Next morning Peckleton tried to put the saga of the robotic tooth business out of his mind. It was an example of double-dealing and dishonesty, but he wasn't sure that anything could be done about it. Still, though, the subject kept creeping back into his thoughts, in spite of his trying to get rid of it. He went outside into the garden and carried on with his work and was busy nearly all day. He planned to do a lot of rooting out, which he always enjoyed, but he found that he was digging on the same spot for rather too long and large holes were appearing in the ground, as he was not concentrating; somehow, he just couldn't settle down his troubled mind.

That night they all went up to bed at much the same time and Peckleton fell asleep quickly, as he normally did. At about 2am he woke up again and started to toss and turn and fidget around. He shook his pillow and tidied up his duvet and then he fell back to sleep again and had a bad dream, the subject of which he was unable to recall when he woke up again, finding that he had a headache.

In the end he felt so fractious that he got up, put on his thick winter dressing gown, crept downstairs so as not to wake the others, pulled on his waterproof boots and, taking a lighted torch, trudged down to the bottom of the garden. He sat down on the old log and stared up at the stars shining brightly in the clear sky and then he concentrated on the surface of the river, which was as motionless as glass.

Just as he was deep in thought, Farallina Fox came jogging along and sat down next to him, as she had spotted a shining torch and wondered what was going on. Farallina looked stunning in the moonlight, wearing her new bright red jogging jumpsuit and matching coloured trainers that she had recently bought from a new sports internet site.

'What are you doing sitting out here all alone, Peckleton?' asked Farallina. 'Can't you sleep? Have you got a worry on your mind?'

'It's not exactly a worry,' Peckleton replied. 'It's a kind of a fidgety thing on my mind, if you know what I mean.'

Farallina didn't really know what a fidgety thing was, so she sat quietly, hoping to get more enlightened.

'I should like to ask you, Farallina, whether you think that mean events left festering without any redress lead to more bad things happening again in the future because the first meanness wasn't zapped on the head?'

'That's an interesting thought,' said Farallina, not a little puzzled by this obscure question.

She wondered whether Peckleton had any particular reason for asking her something so curious and whether he was really feeling quite his usual self, as she had never seen him in this kind of mood before.

'In some circumstances I should say that might well be the case,' replied Farallina, who was keen to get going on her jogging routine, as she was training for the quarter marathon which was happening in the local park next month, and she couldn't see this current conversation going anywhere very interesting.

'Don't you sit pondering for too long and get too cold,' said Farallina, who, before setting off again, gave Peckleton a spare packet of hazelnuts she had in her pocket in case all this contemplation made him feel hungry.

She was humming happily as she went on her way, but she glanced back anxiously at Peckleton a second time before turning the corner.

Just a few minutes later Farallina was back again with Peckleton, sitting next to him on the log.

'That was a quick turn-around,' said Peckleton.

'Actually,' said Farallina, 'I have been thinking over what you just said to me and oddly enough I might have an example of the kind of thing you are on about.'

Peckleton, looking quizzically at Farallina, was anxious to hear what she had to say.

'I had a distressing experience recently that has left me a bit lost for words. It was all rather mysterious. I went to Mr Scammondi Squirrel's dental clinic to have a tooth fixed, as one of mine was in need of attention, and Mr Scammondi Squirrel told me about his new brightly coloured automatic magical robotic tooth replacement machine that he had recently obtained, which he said could remove, design and implant a new tooth, just like that. He advised that it was the only way of dealing with my dental problem.'

Peckleton could hardly believe what he was hearing!

'Yes, do go on, Farallina,' said Peckleton, restless to hear the rest of the story.

'The first treatment went to plan, but shortly afterwards the new tooth started to wobble. I went back to see Mr Scammondi Squirrel for advice, and he said he could put the wobbling matter right but at the same time he said he had noticed that I had developed another problem with the adjacent tooth that also needed a new automatic magical robotic tooth replacement.

'The robotic device put the loose tooth right that I had complained about, and then when it came to replacing the second tooth, I noticed that the robot worked very hastily with Mr Scammondi Squirrel tapping away in earnest at the robotic keypad.

'To shorten the story, Peckleton, this second tooth didn't actually ever show up in my mouth and when I queried it later with Mr Scammondi Squirrel, he was adamant that I had only ever had one new robotic tooth fitted at his clinic – the one that he had put right when it worked loose. I know, though, that I paid for two new teeth, so I have come to the conclusion he had just pretended to install a second one.

'I can only find a single solitary robotic identity tooth glow in my mouth, in spite of my checking with great care for the second one. Mr Scammondi Squirrel was so quick of paw with the mirror when he was supposed to be showing me that second robotic tooth that I couldn't see things clearly. He was very dismissive and hostile to me when I spoke to him about it later and I have felt perplexed and undermined by this whole sorry situation. This is all a bit complicated, Peckleton, but I have tried to explain it as best I can.

'Perhaps that is an example of the kind of thing you are thinking about. I have a hunch that I am not the only patient at the dental clinic to have had this experience, but I don't think anyone wants to talk about it, as it is so embarrassing to be duped in such an obvious way. Oh dear,' Farallina went on, 'I had made up my mind to forget all about it and here I am relating the story to you, and now the anxiety has all come back to me again.'

When Peckleton heard this full account from Farallina he was completely silenced and taken aback. In fact, he very nearly fell off the log in astonishment.

'It is certainly an unusual story,' said Peckleton, finding his voice at last.

He didn't really know what else to say. He sympathised with Farallina, and gave her a reassuring hug, but said nothing to her about Rilganna's experience, as he needed time to think over the whole baffling state of affairs before deciding whether it was appropriate to make any statement about the matter.

'Anyway,' said Farallina, 'I had better get going on my

jogging regime before it rains again, as the wind is changing direction and gaining strength.'

Peckleton, having eaten Farallina's bag of hazelnuts, sat deep in thought for a good hour. That same feeling he had had before when he knew that he had to leave the gang all that time ago had come back again. It was as though he had no say in the matter and that ignoring the situation was not an option. 'I can't leave things as they stand, otherwise I will always feel guilty; inaction in time of need is just as bad as bad action,' he muttered to himself. That didn't sound quite right but he knew what he meant, as he had read something similar in a book a long time ago and the sentiment had remained dormant in the back of his mind, ready as a token of inspiration if ever it was needed.

19

Robotic Investigations

They were all as pleased as ever to see Deptus arrive at the weekend but Peckleton particularly so, as he had something serious on his mind that he needed to discuss with him. It was about the tricky deeds that had been perpetrated at the dental clinic. As far as Peckleton was concerned the disquieting problem had to take priority over replying to Bardwell's letter from the law firm about his unexpected legacy, which fortunately Bardwell had put to one side for the time being to deal with later, when he felt more in the mood for concentrating on it.

Sitting in Bardwell's office on the Saturday afternoon with the door shut, Peckleton went over the saga of the mysterious robotic tooth events with Bardwell and Deptus. He explained about the repeated treatments, the double expense, and the dishonest and underhand behaviour of Mr Scammondi

Squirrel at the dental clinic. Deptus listened carefully to the disturbing tale and was a little shocked. Then Peckleton put forward the idea to Deptus and Bardwell that he had been working on regarding Mr Scammondi Squirrel's automatic magical robotic tooth replacement device. They both paid great attention to what Peckleton had conjured up in his mind.

'I suggest,' said Peckleton, 'that we fix the robotic machine in such a way that its mechanisms don't work properly. Bardwell is a wizard at electronics and with Zig-Zag Pontoon there beside him to give support and advice he could adjust the contraption in such a way that it would create havoc at the dental clinic.'

'But,' said Deptus, looking directly at Peckleton, 'how could this be done? Whatever the circumstances, you can't damage other people's premises by breaking into their property, as you will get into trouble.'

Deptus had a strict code of ethics and breaking and entering was definitely not on his list of doings.

'In any case, Peckleton, it is not fair that Bardwell and Zig-Zag should risk their wellbeing trying to bring this Scammondi Squirrel to book for the bad deeds he has been perpetrating,' continued Deptus, looking vexed.

At this point Bardwell realised that he had no option but to tell Deptus about their unique magical power to invoke invisibility that they had discovered by chance at Waters-edge some time ago. After listening to the explanation of how this had all come about, Deptus said, 'I have only ever known one other who had been granted this unique and privileged gift. Your secret is eternally safe with me, and the revelation will not go outside the four walls that now surround us.'

Straight away there was a shaking of paws all round as an endorsement of trust. Deptus and Bardwell encouraged Peckleton to investigate his plans further and so the scene was set.

Peckleton was unsure whether the magic formula would work for Zig-Zag Pontoon, who had been too worried to try it out when the others did a long time ago, but now, after the fitting of his new powerful AI battery implant to his workings, his resources had been boosted and as a result he had found a new confidence. Peckleton immediately went off to talk with Zig-Zag, who was eager to be involved with the project, once he knew about the extraordinary problems at the dental clinic, so Peckleton went to find the little book of poems and riddles which contained the magical *Instruction*.

Together they went slowly through the conundrum with hope in their hearts and to their great relief Zig-Zag Pontoon was also granted the gift of independent "transitory invisibility", which was then successfully reversed at will with no ill effect. Zig-Zag was thrilled to bits to be such a major part of the venture and so a plan of action could now begin to take shape.

Deptus, with his many contacts in the computer and robotic world, said that he could obtain a copy of the technical manual relating to the magical robotic tooth device, along with the instruments needed to open up its workings and tweak its powers.

True to his word, the following weekend Deptus appeared with all the necessary information and precision instruments in his bag. Bardwell and Zig-Zag spent the next few days in deepest concentration, office door firmly closed, with a "No Entry" sign in place, carefully studying the technical data and electronic diagrams relating to the complicated robotic contraption. They could be heard sighing and talking to themselves as they got their minds focusing on the intricate and complex workings of the device, while at the same time Bardwell was noting vital reminders in his workbook.

***

For a long time Belltring Bulldog had been looking forward to meeting Rilganna, so Deptus, thinking that it would be a good idea if she was at Fremont House staying in the visitor's penthouse apartment while the robotic "remodelling" scheme was underway, felt that this was just the perfect time for her to visit the city of Dunlace and so it was all set up.

Belltring had been waiting for an excuse to do something about Deptus' balcony, which was devoid of flowers and attractive embellishments, and Rilganna's forthcoming visit was a good excuse to take action. Deptus was reluctant to pay any attention to the appearance of his balcony as he rarely went out there, not being very keen on horticultural matters or too much fresh air, for that matter, but it was not difficult to persuade him. Belltring went along to the market and bought some colourful sweet-smelling plants, then she went to the auction rooms and successfully bid for two attractive, ornamental flowerpots and a garden table with matching chairs. She repainted the curved balcony railings a cool and relaxing shade of light green and the make-over was soon done and dusted.

Although Deptus was reluctant to admit it, when he saw the completed job, expedited by Belltring using her natural gifts of colour combination and design, he was pretty taken up with the new look, especially with the arrival of a miniature light-purple flowering lilac bush, the perfume from which he found hypnotic, as most cats do: it had been planted up in one of the spacious new pots that Belltring had obtained and was happily settled into a corner of his balcony. He was pleased that Belltring had gone ahead with her plans. In actual fact she knew Deptus better than he knew himself, and she never would take "no" for an answer when she was sure something was in his best interests, even if he did look a little waspish for a short time afterwards.

Back at Waters-edge, Rilganna, making preparations for her trip, went off to check out her well-worn suitcase. As she peered into the cupboard, she had a huge shock, as her old suitcase had vanished, and in its place stood a smart new travel bag, complete with wheels for easy portability. It had a label attached to it with the words "Have a wonderful trip". Astonished, Rilganna stared for a minute or two, not quite knowing what to do or what to say, but she speedily packed up her clothes, together with her new blue town umbrella, and soon the travel bag was bulging. She hurried back downstairs again when the job was done and thanked them all for the surprise and as they laughed, Bardwell said, 'Most welcome, Rilganna, three times over and more!' and they all clapped and cheered.

At first, she had had no idea where the new travel bag had come from, but then, thinking about it, she remembered that when Deptus arrived the weekend before he was struggling with a very large brown paper parcel that contained something bulky, which quickly disappeared on his arrival. Belltring Bulldog had been busy shopping and had chosen well, as she knew just what a dainty country visitor up to the city would like to transport her clothes in. Deptus, Bardwell and Peckleton had shared the expense with more pleasure than they could have expressed; it was always difficult to think of something special to buy Rilganna for a treat as she was very independent and easily embarrassed by attention.

20

Rilganna's Much-Needed Vacation at Fremont House, and Daxham Helping Out

Next morning Peckleton drove Rilganna to Crindling train station in the Magatt, where she found that her ticket had already been paid for and was waiting for her collection in the booking office. Bardwell, Peckleton, and Zig-Zag, his metalwork glistening brightly in the sun, stood on the station platform as Rilganna boarded the train for the start of her holiday; they all waved her off as the train made its way out of the station and began its journey to the city of Dunlace.

Bardwell felt downhearted and had to quickly wipe away a tear before it dropped down his front and the others noticed his upset. He was being sentimental, because he preferred to know that Rilganna was at Waters-edge; he knew he was being silly and that this much-needed holiday was a very good idea, but Bardwell was not one who liked change, even if was just a temporary arrangement. He couldn't help feeling that way, so it was no good worrying about it.

When Rilganna arrived at the city of Dunlace she was met at the train station by Burgatus Bulldog who, overjoyed to see her safe arrival, soon whisked her off by taxi to Fremont House, where Belltring was thrilled to greet her and even more excited to have her to stay. A memorable holiday had been planned for Rilganna and the change of scene was just what she needed after her recent most upsetting experiences at the dental clinic.

They all had a tasty tea together that afternoon and Albert, now included in all the happenings, joined them too. Rilganna, tired from the excitement of the day, was pleased to have an early night in the Fremont House visitor's apartment. Belltring had placed one of her colourful sweet-smelling flower arrangements in a pretty bowl by the side of Rilganna's bed to help lull her into a peaceful sleep, which happened in no time at all.

The following morning, after an early breakfast, Belltring set out with Rilganna to the well-established fashionable store, Dazzle, Quaver & Soames. For one of Belltring's recent birthday gifts Burgatus had arranged a special account for her and Rilganna to use during their holiday week together. It was valid for purchases in any of the store's departments and had no financial limitations, which was a brave gesture if you think about it! This made trips to the various parts of the store so much more fun for the two holiday-makers as their purchases could be dealt with easily without them having to sort through their purses for their money and credit cards.

Their first destination was the store's refreshment lounge where there were numerous neatly arranged tables, each covered with prettily embroidered tablecloths. Refreshments, including majestically sculptured cakes perched on a delicate white china cake stand, were brought to them in a style of elegance that Rilganna felt she could get used to.

The unusual surroundings in the lounge were a feast of fascination for Rilganna's eyes. She had never seen anything quite like it before. The imaginatively painted walls depicting marble fountains and interwoven garden plants twisting around colonnades in the Roman style were fashioned in soft muted colours. In contrast to the classical there were bright contemporary mirrored friezes fitted all round the room and from the middle of the ornate ceiling hung a huge multi-coloured glass ball, glittering with blazing brilliance as it gently spun around. Rilganna was unable to take her eyes away from the varying styles of decor in the room and had not been listening to anything that Belltring had been saying to her since they first sat down together. Belltring, bemused by her friend's distraction, eventually gave Rilganna a gentle tap on her paw and soon they were both laughing and enjoying the delicious cakes and repeat cups of chilled dandelion tea, laced with lemon, a unique speciality of this stylish refreshment lounge.

With drinks and delicacies enjoyed, they were shortly in the lift on their way up to the hat department and, having tried on a good selection of fascinators, they finally decided on two which complemented them to perfection. They got over-excited trying on the more exotic styles but tried to look serious when spotted by the vigilant sales assistant; it was so hard for them to conceal their laughter as they were having such fun.

Over the next couple of days, the two friends visited some of the famous sights of the city and strolled around the numerous parks and squares. The pièce de résistance was a matinee performance at the Enrapture Showtime Hall on their third afternoon together, when they watched *The Enchanted Swallow* danced by exquisite ballet dancers who made up the City of Dunlace Dormouse Ballet Company.

The captivating music and the beautiful settings were so beguiling that Rilganna drifted off into her own fantasy world. After a little while the two theatregoers were tapped by those sitting in the seats behind them and asked to remove their fascinators, as they were having trouble seeing the stage. The two friends, having arrived at the theatre just in time, had quite forgotten that they were still wearing their elaborate new headgear, both of which resembled television aerials in design, width and height.

Unfortunately, they had spent too long in the city's art gallery, admiring a unique display of rabbit portraiture painted by a mediaeval Italian artist. Then they had wandered around the park, enjoying the colourful seasonal blooms, and dreaming absentmindedly at the city's recently renovated cascading water spectacle as it tumbled down the newly fashioned granite hillside. All this dawdling had delayed their arrival at the Showtime Hall. Fortunately, Rilganna still had her roomy shopping bag with her and as luck had it the fascinators just about squashed into it, with a little gentle encouragement so as not to damage the delicate material, and a catastrophe was avoided.

When Belltring first heard that Rilganna was holidaying

at Fremont House she approached the conservator of the Ancient Sultry Underground Springs for special permission to borrow the Golden Key to allow Rilganna to visit the legendary steamy bubbling wonder. The mysterious site was hidden way below the global crust, not far from Fremont House. Belltring had to make a special case to the conservator through the chairperson of the Official Visiting Committee, and Deptus had to supply a character reference for Rilganna.

It took a week or two before permission was granted, which was by no means a foregone conclusion. Strict protocol had to be followed and Belltring was called upon to pay a large returnable deposit in exchange for the Key. She was only allowed to hold it for a brief period before it had to be returned to the Official Office. She became terrified that she might lose it, so she attached it to a strong piece of string, which she hung around her neck for safe-keeping, just in case it got mislaid.

The Ancient Sultry Springs were of special interest to every Beveranian Rabbit who visited the area, that is, if they were granted permission to view. Without exception, they always found them evocative and a roller coaster of emotion would normally follow a sighting. The learned, well read in such matters, believed that an original community of global Beveranian newcomers had made their first home very near to the bubbling springs, but it was so long ago that it was impossible for any dates to be confirmed; in fact, no one had any idea how many noughts would be required to clarify the situation even if a calculated guess could be made. Quite a few eminent mathematicians had apparently tried to do the calculation and given up.

'I have a surprise for you tomorrow, Rilganna, but we

have to be up and out by 5am, so Albert is going to give us an early morning call so that we don't waste any precious time by sleeping in, as we must not be late. I am not going to tell you where we are going, but you will see when we get there!'

Belltring, having said this, was wondering how Rilganna would react when she saw the ancient waters, so she had some smelling salts in her pocket, just in case she became overcome by the occasion.

When they arrived at the site of the Ancient Springs, Belltring carefully unlocked the old green metal gate with the flat Golden Key, and they climbed down the steep stone steps that were speckled with damp moss. In single file they made their way along a narrow winding overgrown path that eventually came to an end. In front of them was a small grassy clearing, protected on both sides by dense flowering bushes full of yellow and blue chirping birds. The smell of moist fermenting earth filled the misty air and the Warm Sultry Springs, displaying their murmuring magical mystery, bubbled up forcefully from way underground. Rilganna stared into the pool and then her eyes wandered beyond the ancient watery wonder to the enticing thick clover-filled grassy backdrop which, thickly dotted with pink wild flowers, gradually disappeared over the distant horizon.

Rilganna knew instinctively where she was, and so Belltring sat down quietly on the grassy clearing and left Rilganna to enjoy the unique magical experience in her own way, to savour the rarest of moments, and to reflect quietly on the things that were important to her.

As it turned out, there was little time for contemplation as suddenly, and without any warning, a rush of hot air engulfed Rilganna and nearly knocked her over. The misty atmosphere lingering over the pool quickly cleared and a fountain of shimmering golden liquid propelled itself upwards from the watery depths. It rose to a great height before being transformed into sparkling droplets of golden rain as it descended slowly back into its invisible domain in the shape of a glorious golden weeping willow. Sadly, in no time at all its beauty had disappeared, leaving Rilganna in bewilderment with her paws still "glued" to the spot and wondering whether she had actually seen what she thought she had seen.

This special visitor had in fact just received a rare and much sought-after concession. She had been accepted and embraced by the Guild Rulers of the Confederation of the Ancient Sultry Springs who safeguarded the Precious Ancestral Heritage. She had received the Gift of Approval and was surrounded by the warmth and comfort of the Fellowship. It was a rare honour for any Beveranian to receive this inclusion although many dreamed of it.

After a brief lapse of time, not really sufficient for Rilganna to recover from her unworldly experience, a trumpet sounded and a stately voice called out, 'Your appointment is timed out: please vacate the area of the Ancient Sultry Springs, lock the gate securely behind you and return the Golden Key to the Conservator's Office without delay. Be mindful that you are being watched as you leave the area of the Ancient Sultry Springs.'

Before they walked back together to the Conservator's Office, Rilganna, tightly hugging Belltring, said, 'Thank you with all my heart. I will not spend time reflecting on my astonishing early morning as I don't want to bore you with the details.'

Belltring felt enormous pride and was holding back tears with great difficulty.

'I am perfectly content to let the matter rest, dear Rilganna, but if ever you want to talk openly to me about your reflections, I shall consider it a privilege to listen,' said Belltring with great sincerity.

They had missed breakfast because of their early start and so, after they returned the Golden Key (the responsibility for which Belltring was glad to lose), they hurried back to Fremont House for hot creamy porridge followed by several cups of chamomile tea.

With their hunger replenished, the explorers were off out again with renewed enthusiasm. First, they made their way to the Museum of Contemporary Fashion, and while they were listening to a talk and watching a film about "the sensory interpretation of design, shape and colour, particularly in relation to the rhythm of bold and understated structure", Rilganna found herself drifting back to her re-birthing experience earlier in the day. She knew instinctively that her life had been enriched in such a special way that she might never feel quite the same way about herself again.

A little later the two friends had their lunch in the museum's garden cafeteria, with its vivid themed murals painted on the old stone walls. They enjoyed the in-house quartet which was playing and singing with melodious enthusiasm in the courtyard, to all who were willing to listen. A helicopter ride followed in the afternoon, which took them high over the city of Dunlace where they were able to view the rarest of flowering orchids clearly visible through the translucent roofed glasshouses securely perched on the high-rise gardens.

When they arrived back at Fremont House, they found a large parcel waiting for Rilganna. It had been delivered by a special courier while she was out and was very heavy. With encouragement from Rilganna and Belltring, Burgatus set about undoing all the string and tape so that they could see what was inside the stout box. They stared in amazement as Burgatus lifted out a beautifully sculptured golden weeping willow tree, complete with its own stand. At the bottom of the box was a certificate of membership written with great precision in gold-coloured italic hand. Here was confirmation that Rilganna had been officially granted lifelong membership of the Confederation of the Ancient Sultry Springs.

Tears began to tumble from Rilganna's eyes and Belltring made them all a nice cup of tea. What a triumphant end to a magnificent day!

Meanwhile, the normal business of day-to-day activity had been continuing at Waters-edge during Rilganna's absence and there was plenty going on.

As it turned out, it was rather unfortunate that Daxham had been asked to take Rilganna's place in looking after some juniors who lived locally, as their seniors had to be away for the day. The juniors were all to be assembled in one place with their lunch and drinks provided. All Daxham had to do was to keep them occupied and safe, which would seem on the surface of it to be an innocuous enough task.

Daxham didn't want the job at all, and was mightily fed up by the very thought of it, but he agreed, as Peckleton gave him the kind of look that offered him no other option.

At 8am on the Sunday morning Daxham appeared for duty just as the seniors were leaving for their day out on their motorbike and sidecar to join their friends at the yearly meet-up.

Things were going great at first and then after a short while the little ducklings became bored with Daxham's failed conjuring tricks and ceased to laugh at his old jokes, so he organised some games which he had found in one of his many dubious comic books. It was wonderful to see the little ones so happy. Somehow, though, it all got out of hand, and gradually all the juniors got covered in ice cream and chocolate cake, which Daxham managed to find in freezers and cupboards, and the noise got louder and louder. Soon the juniors started to scrap and fight, and the situation became a free-for-all: there was such a dreadful upheaval that poor Daxham was completely out of his depth and unable to settle things down.

Feeling desperate, he telephoned Peckleton and Bardwell, insisting that they come immediately to help in the emergency. It was a good hour before the situation was under control, with the house tidied up and cleaned with no trace of ice cream or chocolate cake to be seen anywhere; finally, peace was restored. It had been a nightmare but when the seniors returned all the ducklings were spotless in their bedclothes and fast asleep. Daxham could never quite explain to them what had happened to all the ice cream and chocolate cake missing from freezers and cupboards!

For some days afterwards, Daxham crossed over the road whenever he saw the seniors approaching, in case they asked him more awkward questions. He decided that he would never again undertake such a terrifying task. From now on he intended to be forearmed, with a list of excuses filed on his smart phone just in case a similar request replicated itself in the future. For a couple of nights, he had some very unsettling dreams, about being locked up in a small cupboard with an enormous sticky chocolate cake which finally exploded, taking Daxham with it.

𝒵1

Challenging Actions, and Returning Home Again

At the weekend Bardwell and Zig-Zag Pontoon spent time putting the finishing touches in place for their assignment at the dental clinic, which was imminent. They didn't want anything to go wrong and so they went carefully over their strategy once again, after which time they finally felt satisfied that they were all sorted and ready for action.

They set off from Waters-edge late on Monday afternoon in Bardwell's cart. They parked inconspicuously under a large sycamore tree, not far from Mr Scammondi Squirrel's dental clinic. Wishing each other luck, they concentrated hard on the magical formula for invisibility that was the first vital link for launching their plans, allowing them to enter Mr Scammondi Squirrel's dental clinic invisibly and unannounced. They deeply meditated on:

A vision of a pond full of water lilies and goldfish, situated in a large field of daffodils, while at the same time gently rubbing his or her head.

They hoped that the magical formula that had worked for them so well at Waters-edge would come right for them again on this most important of occasions.

To their great relief the magical formula didn't let them down and in due course their image began to slowly diminish until they were completely invisible entities.

They carefully locked the cart before setting off to the dental clinic. Bardwell was carrying the technical information and precision instruments in his attaché case and Zig-Zag had their refreshments in a linen bag, both of which had also become conveniently invisible. It would have been a comical sight if the attaché case and the linen bag were to be seen moving along seemingly unaided! They hastened down the street and nervously entered Mr Squirrel's dental clinic. In fact, they had no need to feel uneasy, as they were quite safely shielded by their cloak of invisibility, but it was difficult to feel at ease, as this was an unfamiliar situation and they had yet to gain their confidence.

At the dental clinic things were being tidied away by an assistant, as it was near to the close of the working day. Mr Scammondi Squirrel was preoccupied looking over his list of patients booked in for a magical replacement robotic tooth the following day.

It turned out that the first patient on the treatment list was the chief administrative officer from the nearby city council, a beaver by the name of Mr Rumble. He was a gifted individual, much respected both by his staff and in the wider community. Mr Rumble was in need of a new side tooth. Bardwell and Zig-Zag heard Mr Scammondi Squirrel remark to the clinic receptionist that it was vitally important for them all to impress the officer with efficiency; a satisfied client with such local prominence would do him no harm at all, as words of commendation about him would doubtless fly around the locality like a house on fire.

With all personnel having now left for home the dental clinic premises were locked up for the night.

The computer boffins had a snack, and a cup of tea from their flask, and then Bardwell started on his skilful work while Zig-Zag, keeping very quiet, sat reading his latest robotic journal. The clever badger cautiously unscrewed the back of the robotic device using the precision instruments he had in his attaché case, and with scrupulous reading from his workbook notes, made from their study of the technical manual, he tweaked away at the machine's buttons, sliders and knobs which calibrated and set up the robotic wizard's internal workings, until the task was done to his satisfaction. With a double-check for accuracy having been made by Zig-Zag Pontoon, Bardwell secured the machine back together again and it all looked just as it had done before.

The recalibration project had taken well over two hours and Bardwell was in need of a drink and one or two of his honey and nut biscuits followed by a nap, as he had been undertaking very delicate and intricate work, calling for deep concentration which had caused much muttering; sometime after the task was completed Bardwell was still quietly mumbling as his brain had gone into overdrive and a kind of overheating had taken place.

It did not seem long before they heard the doors of the dental clinic being opened on the Tuesday morning with the arrival of the staff for the beginning of their new working day.

At 9am sharp the chief administrative officer arrived for his appointment. He left his briefcase, hat, jacket and umbrella in the outer waiting room and with a robust paw-shake was welcomed by Mr Scammondi Squirrel. A quite lengthy discussion about the continuing rainy weather followed, as Mr Rumble was carefully settled down in preparation for his treatment.

Mr Scammondi Squirrel, having wheeled the automatic magical robotic tooth replacement device into the treatment area, tapped away at the robot's keypad and it was not long before the robotic wizard began calculating a smart new robotic tooth to be implanted in place of the beaver's damaged one, which had already been magically removed by the device. The patient was completely fascinated by the new brightly coloured robotic machine and watched the activities intently as the robot whizzed, banged and wobbled and got ready to give birth to the replacement tooth.

The new molar started to emerge very efficiently at first, but it began to grow bigger and bigger. Mr Scammondi Squirrel was desperately trying to stop the production of the huge tooth by adjusting the robot's programmable keypad, but the robot was having none of it and the new tooth ended up the size of one that would have been more suitable for a large carthorse, and before long it had grown bigger than the chief administrative officer himself. Not being satisfied with producing one oversized robotic tooth, the robotic wizard started to produce another, more substantial than the one before, and the noise got louder and louder as the robot shook, banged, hissed, and briefly jumped into the air while at the same time making a continuous high-pitched echoing noise, until finally the device stopped doing anything at all, and fell silent.

Mr Rumble, who was normally a calm and well-adjusted individual, began to take fright. He jumped up from the couch with immense speed, and without looking back he hastened from the treatment room and into the waiting room. Having grabbed his belongings he was gone, out of the premises and along the street in no time at all, looking back as he went as though fearful that a huge tooth might be following him along the pavement, and unfortunately his fears materialised. One of the large carthorse molars had grown two long spindly legs with the strength and energy to match; it made its way out of the dental clinic and was pursuing Mr Rumble at a great turn of speed. The terrified beaver was becoming exhausted. He ran into the greengrocer's shop and, shaking like a leaf in a storm, he squeezed into a corner of one of the huge cabbage storage boxes. Mr Scammondi Squirrel, meanwhile, had left the dental clinic and was also hastening along the street: he was trying to catch the huge tooth as it sped along but it was too quick for him. Passers-by were shrieking in horror as they caught sight of the threatening molar but as luck had it the tooth veered into the road and was shattered by a passing car.

A very hot and extremely bothered Mr Scammondi Squirrel returned to the dental clinic in a state of rage. In his anger he started to bang his paws together and tug at his tail: he grabbed the robot's instruction book from the shelf and telephoned the emergency service number printed on the back. He rudely bellowed down the telephone and demanded immediate attention. An hour elapsed before three senior technicians arrived from the service providers. They tried to calm Mr Scammondi Squirrel as they opened the back of the machine. In unison they claimed that the machine had been tampered with and because of this the machine's guarantee was null and void.

The furious dentist emphatically denied that he or any of his staff had ever touched the internal workings of the machine, but it was no good and he had to pay for the device to be repaired and recalibrated; before too long the work was done, and the technicians left the clinic.

Mr Scammondi Squirrel tossed and turned uncomfortably in his bed that night, but he returned to the dental clinic the next morning, quite his usual flamboyant confident self, and continued with his work. As it turned out he experienced three successful robotic tooth delivery days and so he decided to forget the unfortunate event that had happened to him earlier in the week, writing it off as just part of life's unpredictable journey.

Bardwell and Zig-Zag, having left the dental surgery on that Tuesday morning after all the activity was completed, felt thankful when they were able to reverse the magical formula before setting off home in their cart for Waters-edge. Fortunately, the process for the reinstatement of visibility turned out well. Nevertheless, they had nervously reminded each other of the exercise that was involved, so that no mistakes ensued – this simply involved:

Shaking his or her head three times and then rubbing the forehead hard.

How relieved they were when all turned out well to plan!

The activities had been a nerve-racking and time-consuming experience and they were emotionally drained and glad to be back at home. They knew, though, that further action was needed in order to prevent Mr Scammondi Squirrel from continuing to inflict his dishonest deeds on the innocent and unsuspecting, causing worry, sleepless nights and ill-afforded needless expense.

A couple of days later, Bardwell and Zig-Zag Pontoon went back into study mode again to create a new set of procedural data for the forthcoming Friday, when they had scheduled their next visit to the dental clinic. Once again, they had to concentrate hard, working out a new formula from the information in the technical manual relating to the magical robotic tooth replacement device, and it called for further deep deliberation.

Friday seemed to come along quickly as Fridays always do and soon it was time for their second assignment. Bardwell and Zig-Zag inconspicuously parked in the same place, near to the dental clinic, as they had done on the first occasion, and with the magical formula for invisibility having worked perfectly as before they entered the building once again.

It was not too long after their arrival late in the afternoon before all the employees left for home and the clinic was empty. Bardwell once more set about recalibrating the workings of the magical robotic device, which again took two long hours. With the second lot of adjustments finally completed, and with Zig-Zag carrying out his double-check, Bardwell and Zig-Zag began to relax, had their picnic tea which they had brought with them, and took a short nap.

They waited patiently for the time to pass and for the start of the next day when Mr Scammondi Squirrel had another important patient booked in to be fitted up with a new robotic tooth. He was a much-respected local resident, an elderly lion, and the founder member of a large national manufacturing company specialising in non-stick baking tins. Mr Lopham was very particular about his appearance and fastidious about the condition of his teeth. He had been advised by Mr Scammondi Squirrel that he should invest in a new tooth of the robotic kind, as one of his front teeth had become cracked and discoloured.

With a flurry of activity, the patient arrived at the clinic promptly at 10am on the Saturday morning and with all the normal pleasantries and discussion about the continuing wet weather having been dispensed with, the distinguished lion was comfortably settled onto the treatment couch by Mr Scammondi Squirrel, who proceeded to rapidly tap at the keypad of the robotic machine. Before too long Mr Lopham Lion's old tooth had been speedily and magically removed by the automatic robotic tooth replacement contraption, and everything seemed to be going nicely to plan.

As the machine began to go into production to create a shiny new tooth, Mr Scammondi Squirrel started to behave flamboyantly, gesticulating wildly like a conductor of a large orchestra leading his musicians towards the peak of perfection as the robot persevered with its work. He continued to show off as the clinician and the good-natured patient waited for the replacement tooth to appear.

It was not too long before the robotic contraption got very hot and started to pulsate violently, with its aerial spinning at an alarming rate. Suddenly, as if in a great panic, the robotic machine began to spew out a continuous flow of tiny little teeth. It was not long before Mr Lopham Lion, Mr Scammondi Squirrel and the whole room were being pelted by these tiny little teeth, the kind a dormouse might need, or in this case, an army of dormice.

There were so many tiny white shiny teeth on the floor that it was dangerous to take just one small step, as the teeth slipped and slid all over the surface such as small marbles might have done. The patient was totally astonished: he struggled up from the couch with the help of his walking stick, and finally managed to settle his large paws onto the floor, and by moving with great caution he safely manoeuvred himself off the couch, avoiding the storm of tiny teeth as best he could. He had recently been fitted with a new hip and was wearing his soft carpet slippers for comfort. In his condition a fall to the ground would have been completely disastrous.

The patient, incandescent with rage, reverted to his natural instincts, roaring loudly at Mr Scammondi Squirrel in a fierce and angry way. Stumbling awkwardly and quivering nervously he made his way from the treatment room and off the clinic premises. He could hardly believe what had just happened to him. Mr Scammondi Squirrel ran outside to talk to Mr Lopham Lion but all the persuading in the world, and finally the shouting, was not going to convince the patient to linger in the vicinity for a moment longer than was necessary for him to make his escape. Mr Lopham Lion's chauffeur, waiting outside ready to escort him home after his appointment, hurried to assist him. He carefully supported his bewildered employer as he eased himself into the sumptuous limousine and, after carefully placing his woollen rug across his legs, the driver sped off home as quickly as he dared go. Meanwhile, in the treatment room of the dental clinic, the magical robotic contraption, having worked at such an intense rate, was so overheated that it finally let out a great sigh, burned itself out, and gave up where it stood.

Mr Scammondi Squirrel was once more in a fuming state of mind: he kicked out at the robotic device and, as his uncontrolled temper raged, he pulled at his brightly coloured embroidered waistcoat, tearing off the buttons as he yanked and tugged. He telephoned the emergency number on the instruction manual as he had done before but he spoke so abusively to the customer care coordinator that he was cut off from the line and the situation remained unresolved, in spite of his redialling the number several times, as no one was prepared to take the call at the other end.

Bardwell and Zig-Zag having made their exit from the dental clinic, were thankful to return to Waters-edge. A first-class job had been done, intentions had been fulfilled, and they were relieved that the whole trying business was now over and done with.

Back at Fremont House, Belltring and Rilganna had become the closest of friends. They found that they had so much in common: they shared the same sense of humour and were content and relaxed in each other's company and neither looked forward to their time together coming to an end.

On that final Saturday evening before Rilganna's return to Waters-edge the following morning, Rilganna, Burgatus, Belltring, Deptus and Albert had a farewell meal, relaxing together on Deptus' newly organised balcony as they watched the sun go down over the magical River Rushmore. Burgatus toasted their good health and trusted that Rilganna would return very soon to enjoy more of the cultural gems of the city of Dunlace, a sentiment that Belltring endorsed with a great many claps of her paws.

After a hearty breakfast the following morning and with fond farewells and not a few tears, Belltring waved Rilganna off from the large double doors of Fremont House as she left for the train station, courtesy of Burgatus Bulldog driving her in his small city vehicle. Having safely delivered Rilganna, her luggage and the stout cardboard box containing the golden weeping willow and that precious certificate onto the train, Burgatus waved farewell as she began her return journey to Crindling Village.

It was late afternoon and Peckleton was waiting excitedly for Rilganna in the Magatt as her train pulled into the station. How delighted they all were at Waters-edge to see the return of the holidaymaker from Enterprise Wharf. She was feeling and looking so much better for the change of scenery, good food and lots of fun. She had holiday gifts for Bardwell, Peckleton and Daxham and a very special gift for Zig-Zag Pontoon, who tugged off the paper and immediately put on his bright new fashionably styled metal tank top.

The mess-up that Daxham had made of the juniors' sitting job was not relayed to Rilganna, so she was quite pleased with him. Belltring had sent an extravagant box of handmade chocolates, attractively wrapped in colourful paper complete with a large red ribbon tied round the outside, for them all to enjoy in the coming days. Rilganna soon settled back into the daily doings at Waters-edge and how they had missed her company, as their lives had been much diminished by her absence. Bardwell was particularly relieved and happy once more as the balance of his life had been restored.

A few weeks had passed by since the events relating to the magical robotic tooth replacement device involving Chief Administrative Officer Mr Rumble and the eminent businessman Mr Lopham Lion.

One morning an astonished Scammondi Squirrel received a formal letter from the Landsmoth Community Health Agency, which the post person insisted he sign for. He scribbled his name as required and, having hastily torn open the envelope, he was taken aback by its content telling him that a meeting was to take place at his dental clinic the following week on the subject of the Automatic Magical Robotic Tooth Replacement Device. About this he was inwardly confident that he could talk around the situation and get out of the scrape he now found himself in. He thought things would very soon return to normal once he had obtained a new replacement machine and he was certainly not expecting to have to deal with any complications or delays to prevent this from happening.

When the two unsmiling officers arrived on the Wednesday morning, one was struggling with a portable bin on wheels which contained regulations and a casework file containing a large bundle of complaints that had been sent to their office. The senior of the two looked at Mr Scammondi Squirrel in an unforgiving kind of way.

The over-confident dentist asked, 'Would you care for coffee and biscuits, or perhaps something stronger, if you prefer?'

Neither of the two officers succumbed to his friendly approach.

After some official procedures were explained to Mr Scammondi Squirrel in a side room, he was reprimanded.

'You have been tampering with the workings of a delicate robotic contraption, about which you apparently have no technical knowledge, and have caused unnecessary distress to the unsuspecting. I am making particular reference to Chief Administrative Officer Rumble and Mr Lopham Lion, both of whom have reported having to leave your clinic premises in a stressful state of mind and both with a missing tooth, a situation which has not been righted or even explained by you.'

The senior officer who put forward this accusation looked grim and there was not a chink in his unsmiling face. He went on, 'In addition to which, Mr Rumble from the city council had to be signed off as unfit for duty, suffering as he did from horrific recurring nightmares. This condition has only recently been remedied after careful and extended rehabilitation and counselling treatment. The cause of all this stress and trouble was the intense anxiety he suffered at the time of the out-of-control molar incident. It had not been possible to persuade Mr Rumble to leave the safety of the cabbage storage box at the greengrocer's shop at the time of the mighty tooth chase until he had been given a strong sedative by a paramedic. The two patients have since received remedial dental treatment at another clinic and both have now been fitted with correct new teeth, with no thanks to you.'

Mr Scammondi Squirrel, now beginning to see red, was trying hard to keep his unruly temper under control. Trying to put forward a robust argument in his defence he suddenly blurted out, 'This is all exaggerated nonsense. I am a professional serving the community and have been unfairly treated and judged,' but both officers continued to frown and neither looked at all convinced, having such clear-cut and incriminating evidence before them in their files.

Mr Scammondi Squirrel, having been officially cautioned at the end of the meeting, was banned from operating any such apparatus again until he had undergone a thorough period of training and had received the correct certification, which would need to be carefully double-checked for its authenticity. Having handed this ultimatum in writing to Mr Squirrel, the officers left the dental clinic and returned to their office, leaving the dentist feeling furious, having wasted so much time on a non-event, as he saw it.

The automatic magical robotic machine had been manufactured in the Kingdom of Spottilia situated way out across the mighty blue ocean by the Twitch and Domes Corporation, whose works were located in Sunny Creek, Bescara, in Candelessa. Mr Scammondi Squirrel had leased the machine through the company's agents in Glenland, who were the distributors and service providers for the Twitch and Domes Corporation. The executives of the large conglomerate had been agitated to hear about the goings-on at the dental clinic from their Glenland agent and were not at all impressed by the negative publicity that their unique robotic device might receive at the hands of the press as a consequence. They intended to take stringent action to safeguard their reputation.

Not too many days passed before Mr Scammondi Squirrel received the following official letter from the presiding officer of the corporation.

To: Mr Scammondi Squirrel
Regarding Licence 3000-9602: Automatic Magical
Robotic Tooth Replacement Device.

I have received disquieting news from our Glenland agent that you have contravened the terms of the contract between yourself and the Twitch and Domes Corporation by breaking the seals and altering the above machine's delicate settings. This is a serious breach of contract. In addition to which it is reported that you have been verbally abusive to personnel at our Glenland agency while seeking their assistance and have more than once attracted the wrong kind of publicity.

Please note that the above unique licence granted for the operation of our Automatic Magical Robotic Tooth Replacement Device at your dental clinic in the Kingdom of Glenland is hereby terminated with immediate effect, and the severely damaged machine is to be removed from your premises very shortly by our Glenland agent.

You will not be permitted to lease or operate any equipment manufactured by the corporation, now or in the future. Please be clear that there will be no reimbursement of monies appertaining to any unexpired period of the licence that you might consider due to you and indeed you may yet receive a backdated repair bill.

It goes without saying that our chief operating officer is very disappointed with your conduct.

Yours most un-sincerely,
    Signed Dr D Alfonso Browne,
    The Presiding Officer of the Twitch and
    Domes Corporation

22

The Inheritance, Catherton Badger and Trouble With Finances

The dilemma relating to Bardwell's unexpected letter from the Pelliwig law firm in Nimblewissia had not gone away but other more important matters had intervened – namely the dental clinic incidents. Nonetheless Bardwell had been quietly thinking to himself about his land legacy and was now ready to talk about his concerns to Deptus and the others over a cup of chamomile tea and a Chelsea bun, as they all sat together at the kitchen table in readiness for the discussion. They all stared intently at Bardwell, wondering what he might have to say.

Thinking about the legacy land always made Bardwell feel anxious and brought about the nervous tic that had developed in his left eye when the bank shut down and he had to leave his accommodation all that time ago, but he was a courageous badger and so he pressed on as best he could.

'Although it is a bothersome worrying kind of thing that I wish hadn't come my way, I suppose nonetheless that I ought to be appreciative of the legacy gift bequeathed to me by my late Great-Uncle Branchwood Badger, as it was kind of him to think of me and I don't want to sound ungrateful, but I am absolutely certain that I don't want to go into deepest Nimblewissia even to look at the forest.

'To be honest I'm not all that fond of trees *en masse*, although I do like to see the ones in the park, especially in the springtime when they are covered in pink blossoms. I hate the cold and Nimblewissia is renowned for its long fiercely cold snowy winters and nasty keen winds. I don't want to risk my newly found happiness and stability by wandering off, and the very thought of anything other than being here is quite out of the question and makes me shudder in my boots. My home is at Waters-edge with you all and so I think the best thing I can do is to hand the legacy tract of land over to my cousin, once removed, Catherton, and then I can forget that the whole nuisance thing ever peeped over my horizon.'

Having said all this, Bardwell gave a great sigh; however, he looked more troubled now than he did before he started his explanation. This was because he preferred to have his concerns about the legacy filed away in the background of his mind which is where he normally retained them until they started to worry him during the night.

They all remained quiet and deep in thought and then Deptus suddenly said, 'Look, dearest badger, old lad, I think this decision is a bit hasty. Why not take this one step at a time? There is no harm in replying to Percy P Podworthy of Podworthy and Partners of Pelliwig with proof of your identity and at the same time you can ask for some photographs of the land and details about the actual size of the area that they are talking about, otherwise it gives the impression that you are a rather negative dismissive type of badger, which does not look all that good under the circumstances.'

Bardwell had secretly hoped to get rid of the whole disagreeable problem in one fell swoop, but now he found himself reluctantly taking Deptus' advice, so the following week an appropriately worded airmail despatch was sent by Bardwell to Percy P Podworthy of Podworthy and Partners along with certified copies of his birth papers, which Zig-Zag had to get copied at the local general store because the cartridge in their copier ran out of ink at a most inconvenient time, and Podworthy wanted four paper versions as electronic transmission relating to anything legal was unacceptable at the Pelliwig law firm.

It was not too many days before Bardwell received information back in an email attachment from Podworthy, showing the size of the forest tract, along with sample photographs taken from all angles. Bardwell's legacy forest area was enormous and very dense, in fact it was so dark and impenetrable that it appeared to be as black as coal. The girths of the gigantic trees were massive, and the huge structures appeared to reach right up into the heavens above. The residents of Waters-edge and Deptus sat looking at the views in astonishment.

Bardwell, already feeling agitated by this new communication, later received another message and this time it was from his cousin, once removed, Catherton: he had attached a photo of himself dressed in his lumberjack gear leaning against a giant redwood tree in the forest. Daxham could quite clearly see a huge smiling eye complete with long eyelashes set in the bark of the tree just above where Catherton was standing, but he decided not to mention it to the others, as no one else appeared to have noticed it, or perhaps they were pretending they hadn't, thought Daxham, who had recently taken to pondering a little more on things and not jumping straight in, that is when he remembered to.

Catherton was a thickset, strong-looking Nimblewissian badger. He was wearing what looked like an oversized red and yellow checked jacket, thick green trousers, enormous boots and a brightly coloured peaked cap, the colour of which clashed severely with his other clothing. It was obvious that Catherton was absolutely over the moon with enthusiasm and excitement, having at long last tracked down his long-lost Cousin Bardwell, and was keen to build on the relationship.

That night Bardwell didn't sleep very much at all and in the end he got up and made himself a mug of milky cocoa, for he still wished that the legacy land and Catherton would just vanish away, never to return. His tranquil life was all muddled up and Bardwell was not a badger who liked a muddle. He felt irritable because in truth he really didn't want this inheritance that had cropped up. Apart from anything else, he had never been an outdoor badger and was certainly not about to start an outside life now, and the subject just made him feel cross and impatient, both with the situation and with the thought process he had to endure.

After a few days, Bardwell felt he couldn't put off replying to Catherton's email any longer, much as he wanted to. It was inevitable, of course, that his reply would lead to more messages, as the two cousins swapped family history stories, not that Bardwell was able to make much of a contribution as he had been brought to live in Glenland from Pelliwig when he was quite a baby badger, so he had very little to contribute. The communications were tiresome to Bardwell as they took up too of his much time and he found it all rather boring, but as they were electronic, he felt he was able to keep an emotional distance from Catherton to some extent, and he hoped that in due course the messages would fizzle out as communications from long-lost relatives so often do.

Having received the photographs and further information from Percy P Podworthy of Podworthy and Partners, it took Bardwell a little while longer to make his final decision, but he felt it was the right one and so the following weekend he revealed to them all what was in his heart.

'I have heard that many of the wilder badgers living in the area of the Mighty Wooded Badger Plateau rely on the wooded areas for safety and sustenance, and many own exclusive land rights in order to make a living from the forest. I have therefore decided to hand over my legacy land to Cousin Catherton, to continue the estate management that he is already undertaking on my behalf. I think the best solution is for Catherton to keep for himself any proceeds received from this work but with a twenty per cent annual sum being paid to me here, if Catherton can afford it after his expenses, and that way I can remain a "resting" owner. With this way of doing things, everything will remain as it is now, undisturbed.'

Bardwell felt better now that he had this idea off his chest and waited for the others' reaction.

To Bardwell's relief they all clapped eagerly in agreement

when they heard this decision, except for Daxham, who was disappointed and thought that somewhere along the way they (or more importantly, he) had lost a unique opportunity, not to mention an exciting new experience.

Without further delay Bardwell sent off the following e-mail message to Cousin Catherton.

Hi there, Cousin Catherton, it's Cousin Bardwell here. How about this for an idea? Let me know how you feel about this, old fellow. I could pass the managing of my legacy land over to you, in the manner of how things work now. I suggest you keep the annual income that you make and send a twenty per cent annual sum to me, all things being equal, so to speak, and I can stay here and be an executive contributor ready to offer any advice if needed and as required.

Bardwell, having sent the e-mail message to Cousin Catherton putting this proposition forward, was much hoping that the arrangement would be agreeable. Swiftly the following reply came back from Cousin Catherton.

I endorse your suggestion, Cousin Bardwell, with all my heart and with great thanks. I am more than happy to continue estate managing your legacy land. I can tell you are a talented, resourceful and thoughtful badger. You will be included on the circulation list when each year's accounts are available so that you can keep your records up to scratch. This is a most generous suggestion on your part and much appreciated by your affectionate relative.

It was such a relief to Bardwell that Cousin Catherton was in agreement with his idea, and so happily that was how everything went on. The legal documentation was sorted by Percy P Podworthy of Podworthy and Partners with no complications arising and Bardwell felt that he could now forget about the whole thing, or so he hoped.

It was shortly afterwards that Bardwell received another message from Cousin Catherton containing a request that made him feel utterly down in the mouth.

Here I am once again, Cousin Bardwell, Cousin Catherton calling. I have never been a badger who has ever travelled out of his surroundings, but I would very much like to meet you personally, so is there any chance that I could come over to Glenland and stay with you and the others at Waters-edge for a two-week vacation before too long? I am overdue for some hols and am already excited – I could be packed up in no time at all.

Poor Bardwell was horrified. What a bolt from the blue! He rested his head down on his paws and sighed. It seemed to him that matters were getting more difficult and complicated for him at every step of the way, when he had so much hoped that the whole sorry business would just fade away.

When he was at Waters-edge the following weekend, Deptus smiled when he heard about the holiday request as he knew how Bardwell would want to respond.

'I know how you are feeling, Bardwell, old badger, but really you can't refuse Cousin Catherton's request because he is obviously a decent, honest, hardworking Nimblewissian badger, and whatever would he think of you if you made some kind of weak excuse? To make matters easier and to smooth out the problem I can help out by meeting the visitor from the city's airport when the time comes and I'll spend a day or two with him exploring the sights of Dunlace before delivering him personally to Crindling for the start of his country vacation,' said Deptus, who did not really want the job at all but he knew that it had to be done, and seeing the relief on Bardwell's face made his decision and the troublesome aspect of it all the more worthwhile.

Rilganna was so pleased that Deptus had helped Bardwell out with the dilemma of the legacy and the fall-out from it, as Bardwell had become so unsettled by the whole episode and without Deptus' wise advice he would no doubt have been dismissive of his cousin Catherton, the tract of land and the holiday request out of muddle and fear, which would not have been the right course of action.

Meanwhile, at Foxglove Cottage, Farallina Fox was worried and unable to find any peace of mind as she was having difficulty looking after her small investments. The old, thatched roof on her small cottage was beginning to leak and some birds had recently taken up residence in the thatch, so some serious work needed to be done. With the interest rates on her savings being so low and having spent a lot of money on the recent tooth debacle, and with only a limited income to make ends meet, she decided that, when she arrived at work the following day, she would ask Mr Yaxlie Owl whether he could invest her money with more rigour than she was able to do herself.

Unhelpful Yaxlie Owl, after perusing Farallina's small capital sum, politely proclaimed, 'Much as I would like to assist you, I am not able to do so because, as you know, working in my business as you do, I only advise clients with substantial, mainly commercial, accounts.'

After receiving this brush-off Farallina rather wished she hadn't asked the question in the first place. She blushed and felt ill at ease and embarrassed by the awkward outcome and the empty silence that followed.

Yaxlie Owl was in fact rather grateful that this had occurred, as it gave him the opportunity to inform her about a forthcoming change in the office that he had been putting off telling her about, so taking a deep breath he started to explain.

'I know this might come as a bit of a shock, Farallina, but you will have noticed how much my business has been expanding. It has built up to such a level that I can no longer manage the workload on my own, and as such I shall have to reduce your hours of work to half-time to help fund a new accountancy post, as I urgently need to recruit an assistant financial advisor to help me.'

Farallina stared at Yaxlie Owl in astonishment and looked absolutely crestfallen; she was near to tears, which made Yaxlie Owl feel rather ill at ease, but then it suddenly occurred to him that Bardwell might be able to advise Farallina about her financial predicament, and so he suggested that she should call to see him.

'Why not call to see Bardwell Badger for help, for fear not, Bardwell Badger is a very gifted and successful investor,' said Yaxlie Owl. 'He doesn't normally take on clients but as you know them all so well at Waters-edge I'm sure that Bardwell wouldn't turn you away.'

Yaxlie Owl was very pleased that he had thought of this

idea and hoped that Farallina's problem would now fade away as far as he was concerned.

After a few days spent sorting out her paperwork Farallina took herself to Waters-edge one morning and asked to see Bardwell. Farallina had a small suitcase with her that was securely tied round with a stout piece of string to keep the contents intact. It was brimming full as it contained her numerous savings books and financial statements, current and not so current. Bardwell was puzzled by Farallina's request to see him and wondered what she could possibly want, but she came into the kitchen and after enjoying a hot milky chocolate drink and a slice of homemade date cake with them all, she began to explain her financial plight.

When there was a break in her discussion with Bardwell, Rilganna sat next to Farallina and showed her a local newspaper article, relating to Mr Scammondi Squirrel's dental clinic and the fiasco that had occurred due to problems with the workings of the magical robotic tooth implant machine, and the trouble he had got into as a result of his dreadful behaviour. Neither admitted to each other at first that they had both been on the receiving end of Mr Scammondi Squirrel's unscrupulous scams, but both instinctively knew that they had.

Farallina was as astonished by the article as Rilganna was when she first read it.

'My goodness,' said Farallina, 'I cannot help viewing this as some kind of well-deserved compensation, as the terrible calamity it had caused me and, I am sure, so many others sleepless nights and worry, not to mention wasted funds and unnecessary soul searching.'

Suddenly, having finished reading the article, Farallina clapped her paws together and she and Rilganna enjoyed another piece of cake by way of joint celebration!

Bardwell sympathised with Farallina's difficult financial plight after she had explained it all to him, and especially how things had recently gone so wrong for her. As she was Peckleton's best friend, he agreed to take on the task of investing her savings for a modest charge, and gradually her situation improved, in spite of her income having been reduced. Before too long she was able to finance the much-needed re-thatching job on her cottage roof.

Unexpectedly as word got around, Bardwell developed a steady business advising friends and neighbours with modest amounts of money to invest, because they started to come to him for his sound advice and guidance.

After the initial shock, Farallina became accustomed to working part-time instead of full-time in Yaxlie Owl's office. Having discovered that she was able to manage financially much better than she expected, she began to enjoy the advantages that having extra time brought along. She was able to dig and root out at the allotment when she felt like it without being in so much of a rush and she had more spare time for jogging and talking to Peckleton and Zig-Zag Pontoon about horticultural matters and other related things, which made her life so much more rewarding.

23

Cousin Catherton's Arrival at Glenland

Cousin Catherton's visit was imminent. There had been countless face-to-face electronic video meetings of late between the two cousins and it was obvious from Catherton's body language that he simply couldn't wait to board a plane for his forthcoming trip (something he had never ever dreamed of doing before).

They all stood at Bardwell's large-screen processor as he touched base with Catherton for one last time before he left Pelliwig for his momentous journey. Catherton had squeezed his lumberjack friends, who were all wearing very similar outfits and boots, into his log cabin. They were standing together, their arms linked, waving in unison and sending their greetings. Their affection for Catherton was plain to see and they seemed to be just as excited as the new tourist was about his forthcoming trip to Glenland. Catherton was soon to meet his cousin Bardwell and all the others at Waters-edge and Fremont House, and he was over the silvery moon at the prospect.

The journey to Glenland for the traveller was laborious. First, he had to undertake a long, uncomfortable ride in a truck, via very rough, bumpy terrain, from the Mighty Wooded Badger Plateau to the train station at Badger Terminal, and then, having reached the station, there was an even longer train journey before he ever made it to the airport, but finally he did, and apart from a couple of false starts he boarded the right plane and got comfortably settled in.

Catherton was a bit puzzled when he heard the roar of the engines and felt the thrust of take-off, but he soon got over this new experience and, as he was able to fall asleep at the drop of a thimble, he was gone to the world in no time at all. He woke up to enjoy his in-flight meals, although he thought they were rather small, but in spite of this he had two or three large drinks to wash them down. After making a few friendly gestures to fellow passengers, he fell straight back to sleep again.

Catherton didn't have a care in the world; such was his personality.

Deptus had made up a large cardboard notice, with CATHERTON BADGER written in bold capitals across its whole width, which he planned to hold up above his head when he knew the plane had landed and passengers were starting to emerge from the arrivals area into the main concourse. When Deptus spotted Catherton among the crowd of quite a few badgers he couldn't quite believe his eyes, for Catherton was large, well, not exactly large but broader than he had expected, and he took very long strides. To Deptus' surprise he was dressed just as he always was when they saw him in his log cabin on the screen and didn't look at all like a tourist.

Catherton, suddenly spotting Deptus, immediately leapt forward, knocking his cap off at the same time. Then in his eagerness he seized and hugged Deptus so tightly that it left him gasping for breath; at the same time, he trampled all over his cardboard notice, leaving it in tatters on the floor. Poor Deptus was completely winded and knocked off guard.

'So sorry, Deptus, old guy,' said Catherton, reinstating Deptus to ground level and brushing him down, 'but I have been dreaming about this very instant for such a long time I can't believe that at long last I'm actually here with you.'

When Deptus had recovered consciousness, so to speak, they made their way out of the airport terminal to Burgatus Bulldog's waiting car (a small city number) that Albert was driving and they were soon on their way to Fremont House, where Belltring had some delicious fresh sardine and cream cheese sandwiches waiting for them all, along with a substantial fruit cake made that very morning for them to share over many cups of tea, or in Catherton's case, many cups of good strong freshly ground coffee.

It is quite difficult to describe Catherton's arrival at Fremont House, as it was all a bit of a blur. Burgatus and Belltring Bulldog opened the main door as soon as the car arrived, and Catherton's greeting was as hearty for them as it had been for Deptus.

It was obvious that Catherton couldn't fit into the apartment lift if it was to involve anyone else accompanying him, as it was rather narrow and compact, and there was a strict rule relating to maximum capacity to protect the mechanisms. The logistics quickly became complicated and so, after a protracted discussion, they finally all decided to climb up the stairs to the Bulldogs' apartment on the top floor and to forego the lift. Fortunately, as Deptus had already noticed, Catherton only had one small bag of hand luggage, apart from his box of gifts, so getting to the top floor was not too arduous. In an orderly line they slowly climbed up to their destination.

An out-of-breath Belltring, noticing Catherton's heavy boots, asked him to remove them at their apartment door, as stout logging footwear didn't have the kind of soles suitable for walking onto their soft off-white carpeting, and in any case, he could soon put on his carpet slippers. Catherton, however, didn't have any slippers of the carpet variety, or any other kind for that matter, and was a little puzzled as he had never actually heard the word "slippers" before, and was trying to work out what they could possibly be.

A little later, and out of earshot of Catherton, Deptus and the Bulldogs were discussing the awkward problem of the visitor's vacation clothing, or rather the lack of it. Burgatus was worried that the airport baggage section had lost Catherton's luggage at the terminal, but Deptus explained that this was not the case, as it didn't actually exist.

Meanwhile, the new arrival had spotted Belltring's freshly baked fruit cake sitting on the table and, feeling a little peckish and thinking it was all for him, he demolished it in one fell swoop. Oh dear, this was not really a very good start, but it didn't really matter, and Belltring wasn't at all fazed: she was aware that badgers find it very hard to resist fruit cakes and she had another in reserve, which was a habit she had established a long time ago when she was expecting a particular type of guest.

Somehow, they got through that first evening, and Catherton was settled down early to sleep in the visitor's accommodation next to Belltring and Burgatus' apartment, and near to Deptus' penthouse suite. He slept very well and snored all night with such ear-splitting zest that Belltring began to think that a storm was brewing, although Burgatus didn't hear a thing as he always slept very soundly, never ceasing to snore.

Early the following morning Catherton enjoyed his breakfast sitting on the Bulldogs' balcony and fortunately didn't suffer any problems of jet lag or any other similar symptoms that might have caused illness or a delay to the start of his holiday.

Burgatus and Deptus had come to the conclusion that they couldn't deliver Catherton to Waters-edge without anything suitable to wear for his country vacation, and so it was decided that they would take him on a shopping trip to Dazzle, Quaver & Soames to get him fitted out with some casual clothing and comfortable footwear.

The three set out immediately after breakfast with Belltring waving them off at the main door and wishing them good luck. Having arrived at the store they soon found that it was not going to be easy setting Catherton up with a new wardrobe, as there were not that many badgers living in the vicinity of Enterprise Wharf and the choice of clothing was rather limited. Seeing Deptus and Burgatus struggling to find items of the right size and dimension for Catherton to try on, the store manager allocated two personal shoppers to help with the assignment and so Catherton was measured up, down and round twice over for accuracy, and then the conscientious assistants set off to see what they could find in the casual clothes and accessories department that might be a reasonable fit.

It was not a job that could be done with any great speed and so the store manager directed the three customers to the comfort of the coffee lounge, in order to give the personal assistants time to seek out suitable garments, and eventually the job was done. Among the purchases made were practical garments especially suitable for Catherton's stay in the country. The two pairs of casual trousers that he tried on fitted him reasonably well, as they had thick elastic waistbands, and the loose-fitting matching jackets that accompanied the trousers came complete with waterproof hoods, ideal for all weathers.

Catherton was fascinated by the department store and his day out. On his return to Fremont House, after looking through all his bags of purchases, he took great pleasure in showing Belltring his collection of new clothes. So, after a nice warm relaxing soak in the bath, using an extravagant quantity of Belltring's most expensive water-softening foaming bubble bath, Catherton put on his new navy blue and white striped pyjamas, red dressing gown and comfortable indoor shoes. He was spotted by Deptus looking at himself admiringly in the long mirror, which was very reassuring as Deptus so much wanted the visitor to feel happy, comfortable and at ease during his visit, but it was a funny sight, nonetheless.

✐ 24

*Cousin Catherton's Holiday,
and Too Much Lavender*

After an early breakfast the following morning, Deptus took Catherton, decked out in one of the new bright yellow T-shirts and loose-fitting jeans, to the underground station, as there was much sightseeing to be done and not a lot of time to do it in. Catherton had a tendency to dawdle and dream, so Deptus had to hurry him along a bit.

They were off to visit the Puzzling Perpetual Palace.

When they arrived at the reception area of the Palace, Deptus bought the tickets and hired an audio guide to enable Catherton to find out all there was to know about the famous circular tour, which started once they had boarded the mini green train. It promised to whisk them along at high speed while slowing down to a creeping pace at appropriate viewing spots. Unfortunately, the audio guide's earphones didn't quite fit the design of Catherton's ears, but luckily, with Deptus being a master of improvisation, and conveniently finding two elastic bands in his pocket, he managed to fix the problem and Catherton was all sorted in no time at all, with the elastic bands neatly supporting the audio contraption on his ears.

The bouncy circular tour included the renowned horticultural ride of discovery and tropical hothouses. Catherton was fascinated to see the colossal doors automatically open for the little train to make its way through the massive fernery, the giant rhubarb clumps, the huge spiky cacti and finally the tropical camellia groves. The train weaved up and down and in and out as it clattered away on its travels. Catherton got very hot with the excitement of it all. Perspiration was dripping off his nose and ears, but he was not at all put off by this damp discomfort and, while listening intently to the audio tape during the journey, he clapped his paws in earnest, cheering and banging his feet so loudly that it caused other passengers to stare, but he was having such a wonderful time and didn't notice the odd looks that were coming his way. Meanwhile Deptus pulled up his collar, looked out of the window, and pretended to be having a nap.

When the tour was over, the energetic little train went into its neutral position and the passengers disembarked, Catherton and Deptus did the same and made their way through the gate and out into the outside area to enjoy any new attractions that were on offer.

Slowly they struggled up the steep steps to the top of the first high-rise wooden platform they came across. From a great height they could watch the sensational multi-coloured spiralling water show and the surging mini waterfalls below.

When they had seen enough, they had the challenge of climbing back down the long ladder, but they made it, in spite of a stumble or two. They had got quite wet from the watery spray that had blown up onto them, but the warmth of the sun soon dried them off.

Soon they were climbing the next performance platform from where they could gaze down on the delightful fairy glens. The kaleidoscopic displays of twinkling lights spinning slowly around in their cut-glass holders filled the shady rocky valleys with subtle purple lighting: Catherton was in a magical world, for there were so many fascinating things for a badger to wonder at on his first overseas vacation.

Deptus, trying hard to keep to his itinerary, found it difficult to move Catherton on to the next venue as he was more than content to stay in and around the Palace for the rest of the day to listen to the musicians and choirs performing in the Soothing Grotto of Melodies, which unfortunately he had seen advertised on a large notice board just as they were approaching the exit.

Eventually Deptus managed to usher Catherton out and on his way with just enough time for a rapid visit to the city of Dunlace Art Gallery of Classical Masterpieces and then on to the Vintage Transport Museum, where Catherton became animated, roaring with pleasure at the old-style farm and highway vehicles, all of which he wanted to buy to take home. As lunchtime was approaching, they had a short rest at an open air restaurant situated in the middle of one of the pretty grass squares; these green areas were dotted here and there around Dunlace's famous commercial centre and created much appreciated oases in the city centre. Here they shared a barbecued meal of deliciously scented vegetables and nuts wrapped in sheets of soft tasty pasta, followed by two very long lemon drinks served in tall narrow glasses.

With the arrival of a fine afternoon, they boarded the cruise boat that took them on the pre-booked sightseeing trip along the River Rushmore. Along the riverbank Deptus pointed out the names of the various turreted historical buildings, all looking magnificent in the bright sunlight. Catherton, who had bought a camera at the airport shop, had no idea how it worked. He had already lost the box that the camera came in, along with the instruction leaflet. To make matters more complicated, he kept dropping the camera as he excitedly pressed more than one button at the same time, trying hard to hastily photograph all that he could see. A helpful member of the cruise staff came forward to assist with some tuition, and then offered to take a photo of Catherton and Deptus standing together on deck, which turned out to be a stunning reminder of their afternoon outing.

As dusk descended, they joined the thronging crowds listening to the jazz and ukulele bands by the side of the River Rushmore. Catherton downed three large bottles of ginger beer and ate two large bags of Brazil nuts that he obtained from the pop-up shop. He tapped his huge paws to the rhythmic beat and roared with laughter, when he was not occupied with either eating or drinking. He joined in the Frisbee competition that was being organised but was asked to stop throwing so forcefully, such was the strength of his arms and the enthusiasm to win!

As night-time drew near, they took in the amazing views from the city of Dunlace High-Level Spinning Viewing Podium with its super-quick lift and highspeed drone that rendered them almost up to the stars in no time at all.

Catherton was silenced as he had run out of things to say; Deptus was feeling weary and just a little bit dizzy and was looking forward to resting at home, as he felt that he had run several marathons in quick succession!

When they eventually returned very late to Fremont House, Catherton was in a daze and a little over the top with excitement. He wasn't exactly sure where he had been, but he had two big shopping bags full of purchases from the art gallery and museum gift shops that he had been unable to resist, and he declared that he was the happiest badger that had ever existed.

After a large helping of fish pie, which Burgatus had saved for him, and a long glass of tepid chamomile tea to settle his nerves, Deptus went straight to bed and promised to tell the Bulldogs all about the day's adventures in the morning, prior to leaving for Waters-edge. Before dropping off to sleep, Deptus spoke to Bardwell on his mobile to give him just a little advance notice about Catherton's hearty greetings and the state of play to date, so that he knew a little about what to expect!

After breakfast and a catch-up the next morning, Burgatus and Belltring waved Deptus and Catherton off on their travels as the two made their way to the coach station where they boarded for Crindling. Catherton soon fell fast asleep and sniffed and blew loudly throughout the journey. Deptus couldn't hear him; he was plugged in to his favourite rock 'n' roll music via his BD4 player and was savouring the pulsating beat; his imagination was running wild and he was clapping his paws as he had never done before!

Upon their arrival at Waters-edge Catherton hugged everyone at least twice and gave an extra protracted hug to Bardwell. Then Bardwell and he banged paws several times, like badgers do, and Bardwell lost his balance and went down for six, hitting his head on the edge of Rilganna's crockery cupboard. He had to be treated with some soothing ointment, and a large sticking plaster was placed on his left ear by Rilganna, who did not manage to apply it in quite the right spot, and it remained wonky for the rest of the day.

Gradually things (of sorts) settled down a bit, Catherton distributed his gifts and unpacked the one that he had been saving for Deptus; a silk tie decorated with the traditional Pelliwig emblem. For Daxham, Catherton produced a bright green pair of logging boots, dotted all over with small indentations of native Pelliwig leaves, but they were far too big. Rilganna, noticing that Daxham was about to say something ungracious, gave him one of her looks, which fortunately stopped him in his tracks. Rilganna received a gift of handmade Nimblewissian chocolates shaped in the style of the famous Pelliwig leaf which were neatly contained in a locally carved redwood case; Bardwell received a huge pot of rare Nimblewissian honey and Peckleton a pair of Nimblewissian jogging boots, also far too large. For Zig-Zag Pontoon there was a tin of metal polish made from local Nimblewissian leaf-mould and vegetable oil. Upon investigation Zig-Zag found that it had a rather strange smell, so he quickly secured the lid again, as he was beginning to feel a little unwell and so were the others, as the odour emanating from the tin quickly filled the room with a heavy stench that was hard to describe. All the activity became a bit confusing with paper and string all over the place and Rilganna and Bardwell were pleased when everything got tidied away.

Fortunately, a wide-open window soon cleared the

dubious smell that still hung in the air from the Nimblewissian metal polish.

In his gift box Catherton also had a tie for Burgatus that he had forgotten to leave with him when he was at Fremont House – it was very similar to the one he had given to Deptus; he also had a delicately crafted silk scarf for Belltring with similar markings, and there was one for Albert, too, fortunately in a more subtle shade, as being a large Alsatian he was not that keen on anything too dazzling.

Life with Catherton turned out to be fun, although he made a mess everywhere he went, and ate a prodigious amount of food. He loved all his trips out and had many fascinating stories to tell them about his life in Nimblewissia and in Pelliwig in particular. The two cousins, Bardwell and Catherton, caught up with more family matters, although Bardwell hardly knew who Catherton was talking about most of the time because, as we already know, he hardly had any recollection of his early life, but he soon learned that it was easier to acquiesce than to ask too many questions and prolong the deliberations and explanations which Catherton enjoyed making a meal of.

Having accompanied Catherton to Crindling, Deptus returned to Enterprise Wharf that same evening as he had urgent business matters to attend to. He had left Catherton with the prearrangement of fetching him in ten days' time ready for his flight back home to Nimblewissia. As Deptus was leaving Waters-edge for his journey to Dunlace he made it quite clear that he would be unable to visit Waters-edge during those ten days in view of the pressing matters he had to oversee. It was in fact that poor Deptus was worn out and needed to rest up, in readiness to deal with some forthcoming business commitments, as he needed a clear mind and interacting with Catherton was not conducive to unclouded thinking.

As Deptus explained to Burgatus and Belltring on his return to Fremont House, Catherton's main preoccupation was with his log cabin and the trees that surrounded it, the different species, their height, the texture of their bark, and the rate at which they grew. Although Deptus was interested in the subject to some extent, he had reached saturation point regarding wooden structures, their attributes, and the best logs to use for the purpose of building a first-rate wind-proof shelter.

When he arrived, Catherton had given Deptus a substantial volume about Nimblewissia, complete with illustrations, about the fauna and flora of the Mighty Wooded Badger Plateau, which Deptus had placed in the small library in the reception area at Fremont House to be made available for the benefit of any of the residents who were interested, as he was not quite sure what else to do with it.

Rilganna seemed to be forever cooking food and soon found out for herself that leaving a cake, especially a fruit cake, anywhere accessible to Catherton was a huge mistake, but as time went on, they all knew what to expect. They had many glorious and enjoyable trips out together, well, most of the time, anyway.

The visit to the botanical gardens in Landsmoth proved to be a little embarrassing as Catherton, staring up at a huge redwood tree specimen had noticed that something was not quite right with its appearance and suggested that he could trim off a couple of its branches while he was there to improve its future growth. He rested one of his huge paws on the bark of the tree as if taking its pulse and began to frown with displeasure.

Two arborists working in the gardens were immediately called over to account: 'I can see that you are simply not up to the job when it comes to nurturing such a beautiful redwood tree.'

He was about to go on but Bardwell, seeing a very awkward scene developing, swiftly moved Catherton on and into a glasshouse full of colourful flowering poinsettias and toad lilies, while at the same time quickly changing the subject. Fortunately, no serious harm was done, and no apologies were needed or expected by the arborists, who fortunately saw Catherton as an eccentric tourist to be smiled at and jollied along, which was all just as well as it turned out.

The days went by at great speed, and it seemed no time at all before Deptus returned to Waters-edge to take Catherton back to Fremont House to stay the night before catching his early flight home. Catherton's farewell to his relative and friends at Waters-edge was a touching and emotional affair and only those with the hardest of hearts would have been unmoved by the affection they all expressed as Catherton got ready to leave them.

Although at times during his stay Rilganna wished he hadn't been there at all, when it came to saying farewell, she simply said, 'Come back soon, Catherton, a warm welcome is always waiting here for you at Waters-edge.'

'I have had a most wonderful time,' said Catherton, 'quite out of this world or any other world that I have heard about. I am so looking forward to telling my fellow lumberjacks all about my adventures when once again we all sit together staring into the roaring log fire, roasting potatoes and parsnips and singing our Pelliwig folk songs after an energetic day's tree trimming and logging. I shall miss you all so much and a million thanks to you, Rilganna, for all the wonderful cakes I have eaten; I do hope I haven't overdone it.'

With more hugs and with tears beginning to erupt, it was time to go, and Deptus left Waters-edge with Catherton to catch the train back to the city.

Catherton was to come back to see them all again the following year but meanwhile there were regular FaceTime communications to and fro between him and everyone at Waters-edge. Albert had one of the stationery cupboards in the reception area at Fremont House emptied and put to one side in order to store Catherton's vacation clothes, shoes and slippers, so that whenever he came on one of his visits, he was all ready to get up and go.

Life gradually settled back down again after this burst of unusual activity and the little bits and bobs of ordinary life got back on track.

On one of his weekends at Waters-edge Deptus found that he had a different set of bed covers, complete with a new duvet and pillow, which had suddenly appeared. Upon investigation he found that the pillow had been infiltrated by lavender flowers placed there by Rilganna, who had read in her regularly delivered magazine *Robust Health* how beneficial the therapeutic scent of lavender was for hardworking cats of a "certain age". Belltring Bulldog subscribed to the same magazine and she and Rilganna regularly swapped notes on current developments (or fads as Burgatus described them). Deptus preferred his old things; the duvet was homely, and he had liked his well-worn pillow, with its comfortable indentations, and he was sorry that they had disappeared.

Deptus, desperate for advice, asked Bardwell how he could get rid of the new pillow as he needed to get his old one back, but Bardwell was of the opinion that nothing could be done, and he advised Deptus to accept the situation and to make the best of things, so reluctantly that is what he did. He sneezed a lot during the period of acclimatisation but gradually he found he was sleeping more soundly than before, gently dreaming in his restfulness.

Belltring had recently taken to polishing Deptus' furniture with lavender polish when he was away at the weekends, and what's more he now had a flowerpot full of it growing in leaps and bounds on his balcony: he was not quite sure what he had done to deserve all this attention and very much hoped that it would soon be over.

Lavender flowers had also found their way into Catherton's holiday clothes cupboard in the reception area at Fremont House, in order to repel any moths that might decide to take up residence there during the intervening periods between Catherton's visits.

The next week Deptus arrived with a tin of lavender polish from Belltring for Zig-Zag Pontoon, especially formulated to shine up metalwork. Approaching the new tin of polish with caution, Zig-Zag was thankful when he found that it had a more wholesome smell than the tin of polish that Catherton had recently given him, made up as it was from

Nimblewissian leaf-mould and vegetable oil. Peckleton now had that version stored in his garden shed, with the intention of putting it on the ground near to his vegetables next season to dissuade slugs and snails from eating the tender shoots.

$\mathcal{25}$

Serious Trouble Afoot

It was a lovely warm day and Deptus, down as usual for the weekend at Waters-edge, was resting in the garden hammock, secured as it always was between the weeping willow and the old, twisted apple tree. Peckleton had been gardening all day, Bardwell was busy with his financial dealings and Daxham was reading an article in one of his magazines that offered the prospect for learning more unreliable conjuring tricks. Rilganna had planned for them all to assemble on the lawn in the afternoon to have their tea together in the late autumn sun.

During the course of their usual chattering over the picnic tea, Daxham suddenly said, 'I was talking to Billie Badger today and guess what he told me?'

The others were just a little irritated by this remark, as how could they possibly know what Billie Badger had said!

'Well, what did he say?' said Peckleton, asking what the others were all thinking; they all waited in anticipation, especially Zig-Zag Pontoon, who was very interested in anything that Billie came up with as they often played dominoes together.

'Billie Badger said that he had heard from a very reliable source that the Scoodles at the Ultor Commune where Rilganna used to live were pulling out to move westwards down towards Flux in the next ten days, and that they had found out where she was living.'

'Are you absolutely sure that you heard this correctly?' asked Bardwell, with urgency in his voice.

'Yes,' said Daxham, 'I'm positive I heard this right.'

Rilganna immediately began to feel unsteady and concerned.

Daxham felt important, as it was not often that he said something that anyone took that much notice of.

Deptus was immediately alert, and everyone stopped eating, for they knew that Billie always had his ear to the ground. A cold rod of steel shot through Deptus because he was sure that the Ultorian Elderians would not leave Crindling without planning to take Rilganna with them. She had been too useful to them in the past: they had only realised that after she had been so cruelly dumped by them all that time ago, and they had been searching for her ever since.

After hearing this unwelcome news, none of them had much of an appetite for sandwiches and trifle, but somehow, they managed to eat up their picnic tea, as they didn't want to worry Rilganna more than was necessary by acting any differently to usual. Shortly after tea they all went indoors and sat in Bardwell's office together, while Rilganna was reading her new book at the kitchen table.

Deptus' mind was working at high speed.

'I'm returning to Enterprise Wharf early,' said Deptus. 'In fact, I'm going now.' He turned to Peckleton and said in a hush, 'Rilganna must not go outside under any circumstances, and all the doors and windows must be kept fully bolted day and night.'

Peckleton looked penetratingly towards Deptus as he instinctively understood only too well what danger was lurking.

'I shall return the day after tomorrow with six companions,' said Deptus, 'and by then I shall hope to have a plan of action to counter this malicious threat.'

Deptus made a hasty retreat, catching the next fast train back to the city of Dunlace, and speedily made his way to Enterprise Wharf and Fremont House. On his arrival he told Burgatus and Belltring what had transpired and the danger Rilganna, and probably the others too, were now in. After a quick snack and a warm drink Deptus filled his hot water bottle and went to bed, but it was hard for him to rest as his mind was lit up like a firework.

Next morning Deptus was up at the crack of dawn, having had his brain buzzing away all night with plans for the day to come. After a quick bowl of creamy porridge, and a splash of cold water on his face to brighten his brain, Deptus made his way by underground train to Gardenia Row and to the eminent jewellers Shred and Bows. He needed to talk to his old friend Ms Alicia Peacock. He had already texted Alicia, as no one was permitted to enter the prestigious firm of Shred and Bows without a prearranged appointment, and

Deptus wanted her to know that he was on his way. Apart from being a jeweller of great repute, Alicia was a hot shot on knots and twines: there was no one in the city of Dunlace who knew how to tie everything up in knots at breakneck speed like Ms Alicia Peacock.

Over the years Deptus and Alicia had supported each other on many a venture and, realising that something very serious must be in their midst, she listened carefully to what Deptus had to tell her: without a second's hesitation she offered Deptus the full scope of her expertise to help counter the malicious threat.

'Whatever it takes, Deptus, I shall be right there beside you. I have experienced bullies in the past and have no time for such hateful behaviour,' said Alicia, with a passion that was no surprise to Deptus.

Having handed him a small cardboard box containing a large apple turnover and a bar of creamy chocolate to keep up his energy levels, she said farewell to her friend and ally and went off immediately to the stockroom to check on her assortment of scissors, tweezers, twines, bodkins, yarns, buttons and pegs.

As time was getting on, Deptus went by taxi to visit his greyhound friends, the owners of an unconventional hotel in Topaz Row called The Bottomless Bounce. Lorum, Nailey and Deptus had shared tough times when the two greyhounds were having to race for a living and Deptus wasn't sure where his next plate of fish was coming from. The three had always stood shoulder to shoulder in times of trouble and strife.

While they sat together in the elegant kitchen-cum-diner of The Bottomless Bounce, enjoying a sustaining bowl of fish soup, a large warm bread roll and a freshly baked spiced bun, Deptus told them about the disturbing problem that had just arisen, while at the same time contemplating what risks might lie ahead. Having listened closely to the story, Lorum and Nailey confirmed that they would be fully up for the forthcoming onslaught; this was a great boost for Deptus as Lorum and Nailey were shining lights when it came to tactical manoeuvres. When it was time for Deptus to say his farewells, Lorum and Nailey gave Deptus a hearty pat on the back, telling him not to worry, and promising him a first-class celebration lunch in their hotel dining room once all this terrible trouble was all done and dusted.

Deptus had to make one more visit, which involved boarding a boat, as he needed to talk to the captain, Dizz, and his first mate, Des, on one of the River Rushmore's finest luxury leisure cruisers, *The Deep Blue*. First Deptus needed to text Spangles Sarno, a large, majestic seal, who now preferred river life to a life on the ocean wave, and was Deptus' much-loved fishing companion. Spangles Sarno had his tender close at hand to give Deptus a boat lift to enable them to board *The Deep Blue*. Having received the text from Deptus sent direct from the bank of the River Rushmore, Spangles Sarno was there at Deptus' side before you could say "grilled haddock" and was able to row them out across the river to Dizz and Des' waiting cruiser in no time at all.

On arrival they were speedily winched up onto the deck of *The Deep Blue*, leaving Spangles' tender safely secured alongside Dizz and Des' magnificent vessel in readiness for their return journey. Spangles, who had already committed his services to help Deptus see off the wicked enemy, had a loud-hailer which he was to bring along to Waters-edge in case any instructions, warnings or battle cries were needed to be broadcast during the forthcoming offensive.

Deptus and Spangles Sarno had once helped protect the two ginger cats Dizz and Des when they were being attacked by a gang of nasties late one night in Bradley Cross, as they were passing by a public house frequented by the marine fraternity, and from then on the bond of friendship with the two had been as firm as a docker's handshake. The cats, after hearing the story, confirmed without hesitation that they were "on board"; they were already up and running, full of zeal and keen to get going.

Deptus' next move was to collect the brass barrel blunderbuss he kept in his lock-up near Hadden Hippo's garage. Some time ago Deptus had had his blunderbuss altered and now it had a back-end pump action attached to a wide receptacle large enough to hold a substantial tin of paint. Deptus had taken the opportunity to test this out no longer than a couple of months ago and the blunderbuss had efficiently exploded the paint in a great burst of colour. His next stop was the warehouse on the corner of the next street where he bought six tins of indelible red paint to be express-delivered the next day to Waters-edge.

An exhausted Deptus eventually returned home, briefly bringing Belltring and Burgatus up to speed on the day's developments, then he had a light supper and went to stretch out on his bed, knowing that he had a very early start in front of him the next morning. In his mind's eye he had already worked out a strategy for the next few days and spent some time visualising what might lie ahead. Make no mistake, Deptus knew they all had to be very brave.

From his own experience of life, Deptus was well aware

that nothing worth having ever came easily, and what was more valuable than Rilganna's life and freedom, which was now under threat.

Deptus was fired up bigtime and when he got fired up he was one of the most single-minded and determined cats you ever would find in the city of Dunlace, or anywhere else for that matter.

26

Plans Are Made

Early the following morning, Alicia, Lorum, Nailey, Dizz, Des and Spangles Sarno were waiting for Deptus at the coach station, when he arrived with his blunderbuss in a big metal box; the box was very heavy and had slowed his pace down quite a bit. Alicia had with her a capacious bag full of multifarious twines, yarns, tweezers, pegs, buttons, needles, pins, scissors and pattern books. Belltring and Burgatus Bulldog had sent along a basket packed with sandwiches, breakfast snacks and a large flask of tea, enough for all seven of them, and as they winged their way out of Dunlace and into the countryside they enjoyed their picnic breakfast sitting in the comfortable coach discussing the forthcoming plan of operation.

When they arrived at Crindling village they disembarked from the coach and made their way to Waters-edge.

Peckleton, who had been alerted by a text from Deptus about their imminent arrival, was ready by the front door to unlock and welcome them in. Rilganna, Peckleton, Bardwell, Daxham and Zig-Zag Pontoon were relieved to see Deptus, all the boys and Alicia; Alicia was over the moon to meet Rilganna and Zig-Zag Pontoon, both of whom she had heard so much about. She gave Rilganna an enormous embrace and told her not to worry a tipple.

After settling in, the visitors and the Waters-edge residents sat at the kitchen table enjoying homemade vegetable soup, crusty bread rolls, cheese and numerous cups of hot chocolate (all except for Zig-Zag who just swallowed his usual AI vitamin pill. However, he always enjoyed helping to serve up the food and watching others eat it).

They discussed their forthcoming plans, agreeing that the Ultorian Elderians and the Scoodles from the commune would most likely attack within the next day or two. It was therefore decided that Alicia would knot and bind up all the downstairs windows in her inimitable way, thus rendering them completely impenetrable from the outside. Peckleton and Zig-Zag Pontoon were both to be on upstairs watch at Waters-edge – a precaution, just in case one of them nodded off! With the use of Peckleton's excellent high-strength infrared binoculars they would be able to see from a distance what was going on at the Ultor Commune and would know when the Ultorian Elderians and the Ultorian Scoodles were on the move.

As soon as Peckleton and Zig-Zag Pontoon saw activity in sight and had alerted the others, Rilganna, Alicia and Daxham would be in charge of filling buckets of cold water from the bathroom tap, ready to shoot down on the enemy from the upstairs windows. On her way up the spiral staircase behind the other two, Alicia was to knot and twine up the staircase as she went, so that the evil enemy, if they got inside Waters-edge, would be unable to make their way up the stairs and kidnap Rilganna. Provisions were already stored in one of the bedrooms in case of a siege that went on for longer than expected.

In truth none of the Waters-edge residents, nor Deptus, Alicia, Lorum, Nailey, Dizz, Des or Spangles Sarno knew what to expect, but they were as prepared as they could be for whatever fate had in store for them.

At 5pm Deptus suggested that they should all try to rest up, so that their minds and bodies were as refreshed as possible for the forthcoming challenge, and so Peckleton and Zig-Zag took up their position at the back window.

Suddenly at midnight, Peckleton and Zig-Zag let out a great shout, in unison. There were carts being shunted around; they could see the Ultorian Elderians and the Scoodles skulking about in the darkness.

With Deptus, Bardwell, Peckleton, Zig-Zag Pontoon, Lorum, Nailey, Dizz, Des and Spangles Sarno now assembled downstairs, Alicia started to seal off the staircase with her intricate web of knots and twines as she, Daxham and Rilganna slowly climbed up the stairs.

They did not have to wait long before three muddy old carts sped into the courtyard, causing gravel to fly up into the air; their brakes screeched loudly as the vehicles suddenly halted. Four tough-looking Ultorian Scoodles jumped out from each of two carts, and four Elderians (senior Ultorians) jumped out from the third one. They were all scruffily dressed, their torn jackets filthy dirty and their boots worn down and much the same.

The biggest of the pack, the Chief Elderian, by the name of Mould, banged noisily at the door of Waters-edge while the others stood back. To the Ultorians' astonishment the door quickly flew open and Deptus stood in the doorway. Next to him on one side was Spangles Sarno, firmly clutching his loud-hailer, and on the other side stood Zig-Zag Pontoon, wearing the formidable coat of shiny armour that he had recently bought from an advertisement he had seen on his on-line robotic magazine site. The two sturdy cats Dizz and Des stood just behind, then to the rear of Dizz and Des stood the two nifty greyhounds Lorum and Nailey and finally, last but not least, stood Bardwell with Peckleton.

With cold piercing eyes, Mould, acting as spokesman, stared maliciously at Deptus while at the same time hissing in a sinister fashion; then in a gruff threatening tone, he suddenly said, 'We want no trouble from you or with you, but we demand Rilganna back. She has always lived at the commune.'

Deptus laughed in his face, and then growled fiercely, like cats do when they are very angry. His top lip curled up, which made him look as if he meant business, and lifting himself up to his full height he said, 'Every soul is free to walk the earth and at liberty to choose his or her own destiny. Rilganna belongs nowhere; she alone decides where she stays and what she does. You have spent too much time mouldering underground, Mould, you lost the plot years ago!'

Mould was furious. His mean little eyes squinted, and he started to tap the rod he was carrying against his bulky thighs.

'I have noticed that the arrogant always tap something,' said Deptus, 'perhaps a teaspoon, a pen or a ruler, sometimes a twig and in your case a rod.' At this remark all the Waters-edge crew began to laugh mockingly.

Deptus and Mould continued to stare unflinchingly at each other.

The Ultorian Scoodles, still standing further back from Mould, were waiting for a sign to attack, which they now had from their leader, who raised a sinewy forearm: they began to move forward and brandishing their clubs, rods and twisted pieces of gnarled wood they now stood close by, eager for combat.

The Waters-edge contingent was up against it, but they had nerves of steel and unbending fortitude on their side. Suddenly all the Ultorian Scoodles charged together with their fearsome weapons. Egging them on, the Ultorian Elderians stood on the sidelines, ready to resharpen the attackers' sticks if they were damaged and blunted in the struggle.

Miraculously the enemy were kept from getting over the threshold of Waters-edge as Lorum and Nailey put into action their meticulously practised combat manoeuvres that they had gleaned from an old military textbook they found up in their attic at The Bottomless Bounce. The first one to be struck on the head with a club by an Ultorian Scoodle was Dizz, who was not at all dizzy as a result because under his woolly hat he had a thick helmet of steel and as the club hit his hat, it rang out with a deep bell sound.

Des began his well-practised *tai chi* movements while making use of a hefty branch from the old apple tree, knotted as it was with sharp shoots sticking out all the way down.

As he moved towards the hostile Scoodles with slow drawn-out steps and strides, graceful movements and rotations of the body, followed by rhythmic arm movements, pulls and pushes, and wearing the scary mask brightly painted with a weird expression that Dizz had made especially for the battle, it somehow temporarily unnerved the ruthless enemy. Deptus, Spangles Sarno, Bardwell, Peckleton and Zig-Zag, armed with large stout saucepans and lids, charged for all they were worth. The Ultorian Scoodles did their best to unsteady Zig-Zag Pontoon but with his suit of armour too sturdy to upset his balance the robot continued edging purposely towards the enemy with an unswerving motion.

Upstairs at Waters-edge Daxham and Rilganna had been busy filling up buckets and bowls with cold water from the bath tap. Rilganna was keeping well away from the window so that her position was not visible to the Ultorian Scoodles below. With buckets and bowls now lined up and full to overflowing, Ms Alicia Peacock attached the water hose to the bath tap; they were ready for action.

The upstairs windows suddenly flew open and cold water sped down from the upper reaches; the hose pipe at full pelt added to the downpour. Nonetheless things were not going well, for all the Waters-edge defenders' bravery, as another two carts containing eight more of the heavy mob arrived at the battleground. They jumped out of their vehicles and moved steadily forward: they had been sent as reinforcements, ready to take action if things didn't go Mould's way and the Waters-edge cohort were not the pushover that he had expected them to be.

It was now a battle royale with clubs, sticks, rods, branches, saucepans, lids and cold watery contents shooting everywhere. Bardwell and Peckleton were knocked to the ground but Dizz, Des, Lorum, Nailey, Deptus, Zig-Zag and Spangles Sarno, somehow managing to shout abusive insults through his loud-hailer, kept going against all the odds.

Nearby, the Magatt, tucked away in her shed, was becoming more and more irritated. She had been awakened from her peaceful sleep by a war-like uproar emanating from the yard outside and was far from pleased. Suddenly her patience broke. The shed door flew open, making a loud banging noise; the Magatt discarded her blanket as she shunted herself out into the open. Her Azure Blue paintwork had changed from its deep hue to a vivid and pulsating shade of orange, her lamps were now ablaze, flashing intermittently, and her horn was sounding loud and furious in the darkness of the night. With determination fuelled by annoyance she careered towards the Ultorian Scoodles, and the spiteful enemy were forced up against their carts. They were blinded by her penetrating lamps and disorientated by the sound of her angry engine, which was accelerating loudly and becoming and more and more irascible by the minute.

Meanwhile Deptus, helped by Des and Dizz, hastily fixed a tin of the indelible bright red paint onto the receptacle of the brass-barrelled blunderbuss. The Magatt, having backed the dreaded Ultorian Scoodles into one area, once more concentrated her blazing lamps straight onto them, thus disabling any opportunity they had for counter activity. The three Waters-edge warriors carried the blunderbuss out into the open and pulled the trigger. At the same time the Magatt reversed herself out of harm's way to avoid any nasty red splashes getting onto her shining bodywork. The Ultorian Scoodles, pelted with the bright red paint, stared in bewilderment as they tried to work out what it was. Deptus coupled up a further tin of paint to the blunderbuss and fired again; a couple of further thrusts covered the Scoodles' carts in the same red liquid.

Deptus, using Spangles' loud-hailer, shouted to the Ultorian Elderians and the Scoodles in a forthright and forceful manner, his free paw clenched in defiance.

'Get all your junk packed up, loaded, and be moving westwards from Crindling down towards Flux within the hour, taking your climate of open hostility with you, never to return. We shall be watching and waiting, and make no mistake, we shall win this battle.'

The cruel and wicked enemy was in fact defeated, and the conflict was over. Mould, the rest of the Ultorian Elderians, all the Scoodles and their respective carts covered in the dripping red paint made their departure from Waters-edge, but not without bellowing out empty malevolent threats as they drew away in disarray.

While this final activity was being enacted the Magatt reversed herself into the shed and calmly turned off her engine and headlights. As Deptus walked towards her he noticed that her bodywork was slowly reverting from the pulsating shade of orange that she had adopted for the battle back to the more refined Azure Blue. He covered her over with her night-time blanket, and by the time he had done this, and had told her how very brave she was and how she had saved the day so triumphantly, she had already fallen fast asleep. He switched on the warm-air heater that stood in the corner of the shed and shut the doors, leaving her alone to enjoy a well-earned rest, as all the sudden activity and the disturbed night had completely worn her out.

27

What a Relief

As the Ultorian Elderians and the Scoodles were travelling back from the battle site to the Ultor Commune, they were spotted by Joseph (one of the residents from the Challion Community) returning home late from a rock concert with Billie Badger and Farallina Fox. The three, feeling rather tired, rubbed their eyes because the sighting they had chanced upon in the light of the moon was so extraordinary. But no, they were seeing straight, all the Ultorians' carts, the drivers and the passengers were dripping in bright red paint.

Joseph immediately rushed down the main entrance of the Challion Community network and woke up all the locals, who straight away jumped up out of their bunk beds and spread the astonishing news throughout the surrounding neighbourhoods. Before very long it had permeated into the community's deepest burrows which were widely spread under the hillside's subterranean networks.

Still in their nightclothes, the clan communities surfaced *en masse* onto the hilltops, gazing unbelievably at what they saw. They continued to stare in astonishment as the Ultorian Elderians and their associates pulled out from their commune within the hour, leaving much bad feeling behind them. There was utter relief and rejoicing at their departure; it was like a dream come true. Suddenly, a solitary clap was heard which very quickly spread and before long spontaneous laughter and cheering broke the stillness of the cold night air.

It was these local clans who had named the inhabitants from the Ultor Commune "Scoodles", because of their despicable, greedy and hostile activities: in the local Challion dialect "Scoodles" means just that.

Meanwhile at Waters-edge, Alicia began unpicking and detaching her tightly tangled pattern of twines, yarns and knots with great dexterity as she came down the stairs, with Rilganna and Daxham patiently following her.

Rilganna was so completely overwhelmed and bowled over with relief at the miracle that had occurred that she found it impossible to think of the right words to explain how she felt. Above all else she knew that she would now be able to live without fear. For as long as she could remember she had leapt up in terror when she heard a bumpy noise in the night, and now she could put the memory of the loathsome Ultorian Elderians and Scoodles behind her.

How they all rejoiced at Waters-edge as no one was badly hurt. With careful planning and courage and with the help of the fearless Magatt they had put down wickedness and evil, and they all agreed that the bruises, cuts and bumps they had sustained had already been soothed with the contents of Rilganna's first aid box newly replenished for the battle.

To take Rilganna's mind away from the emotional upheaval she was experiencing, Deptus told her that he would mix up some strong anti-stain solution to get rid of the bright red indelible paint which seemed to be all over the place, and they all laughed and clapped. Alicia, who was a pleasure to be with, promised to release her amazing labyrinth of complex twists, twines and knots from the downstairs windows before she left, as no one else at Waters-edge would have known quite how to tackle it. They all agreed that they had never ever seen such complex shapes and criss-cross designs as Ms Alicia Peacock was able to stitch together at such an astonishing speed.

It was no mystery why Alicia was in such great demand for her intricate and bespoke jewellery designs. Her work was much sought after, by wealthy celebrities and the well-to-do from all over the world, who enthusiastically endorsed her extraordinary talent: they would wait patiently in turn to be in possession of one of her stunning delicate creations. Alicia only accepted a limited number of commissions each year and her beautiful jewellery was made all the more precious by the rarity of her work.

Early the next morning Farallina Fox and Billie Badger hastened along to the Swanningbell Mill Hotel on Billie's motorbike to tell Jeremiah Swan about the battle and the goings-on from the night before. Mr Swan, eating breakfast at his usual table by the bay window, put down his large cup of steaming tea and sat motionless as he digested the news.

'This is the time for an elaborate celebration with no

expense spared,' he exclaimed, and having recovered from the shock of the extraordinary report he had just been given, he once again tucked into his wholemeal toast and lime marmalade. Farallina and Billie were asked by Jeremiah Swan to return to the Mill at 2.30pm that very afternoon to collect invitations from him to deliver to Waters-edge.

Alicia, Lorum, Nailey, Dizz, Des and Spangles Sarno, having stayed the following day with their friends, were overcome with surprise and pleasure when they, along with Deptus and all the Waters-edge residents, received personalised invitations from Mr Jeremiah Swan specially hand delivered by Farallina and Billie.

You are invited to attend a celebration dinner this evening to be held at the Swanningbell Mill Hotel starting at 7pm sharp on the dot – dress casual – mood relaxed. RSVP to Jeremiah Swan Esq by return.

Farallina and Billie returned immediately to Mr Swan carrying a speedily produced card of acceptance.

At 7pm Jeremiah Swan, his feathers freshly powdered and resplendent in his black silk evening jacket, deep blue cummerbund, spotless white shirt, and light-blue and white spotted bow tie, stood at the main door of the hotel to greet all his guests with a hearty slap on their backs, words of congratulation, and a glass of the very best strawberry wine and cordial poured by Farallina, Billie and Joseph, who were assisting Mr Swan with his hosting duties and included as guests at the celebration.

A beautifully decorated private room had been set aside

at the Mill for the occasion and the Swanningbell's superb china, glass and brightly polished cutlery and decorative silverware were meticulously laid out with military precision on the top of the huge trestle table, festooned as it was with an immaculately starched and pressed white linen table cover. Tall blue candles flickered from their sturdy solid silver holders; the oak-panelled walls, the sumptuous red carpet and the stunning gold-framed paintings looked magnificent in the candlelight, and relaxing melodic music filled the air. The ambience of the room was perfection itself.

Without any delay, all the guests were comfortably seated, and the gala evening commenced.

As the sweetest of champagnes and aromatic fruit juices flowed, they all gasped with appreciation, as the chefs produced examples of their very best dishes. Wearing his tallest torque and necktie, Wilfred Samphire (a seal and international fish chef of renown who had learned his trade in the far-off islands of the Sparkling Green Ocean), having heard that Spangles Sarno was joining the celebration, had cooked a delectable cod fillet especially for him, garnished with a sauce prepared to perfection containing chopped onions, fresh parsley, lemon juice and two other secret ingredients. This delicacy was proudly delivered with stately panache on a silver platter by the fish chef himself.

Spangles Sarno, quite overcome with a combination of honour and delight, stood up from his seat to rapturous applause and offered his heartfelt thanks; tempted though he was to swallow the delicious delicacy in one huge gulp, he sat down and ate with the gracefulness and decorum that he felt the opulent occasion called for.

A more joyous occasion with livelier conversation could

not have been imagined. Sitting next to Jeremiah Swan, Daxham was allowed as much ginger beer as Rilganna would allow him to drink. Finally, at the end of the dinner, as the sweet dessert wine flowed, and with the chocolate trifle having been eaten, a delicately iced sponge cake encircled by richly filled white truffle chocolates, which Rilganna had ordered earlier from Bings Bakery, was delivered to the Swanningbell Mill. The celebration cake was decorated with twinkling multi-coloured sparkling candles which surrounded a tall musical singing candle which was perched in the middle; to roars of delight these items of beauty were all spontaneously encouraged into action by Jeremiah Swan in the darkness of the room. Zig-Zag Pontoon's metal bodywork and new tank top, polished to perfection with Belltring Bulldog's lavender polish, gleamed like a bright planet at the far end of the table.

So overwhelmed by the sense of occasion, the guests all shouted in unison, 'Ha rah,' 'Ha rah,' 'Ha rah,' and they all shouted the same again, again and again, paws, flippers and wings banging loudly. Bardwell stood to offer a memorable speech in praise of every single one of them. Great appreciation was offered to Jeremiah Swan for hosting such a wonderful event and special thanks for their great bravery were expressed to Deptus, Alicia, Lorum, Nailey, Dizz, Des and Spangles Sarno, for without them they might not have been celebrating in this most memorable way. The Magatt was not forgotten and was toasted and cheered in her absence.

Rilganna, at times such as these, when candles flickered and the illumination was hazy, found herself involuntarily recalling the dreary yellow light that the infrequent wax candles had created in the dimly lit tunnels of the Ultor

Commune all that time ago. They were unwelcome recollections, but memories of that gloomy setting were no longer any cause for fear. She now felt that she could face them head-on and would soon be able to obliterate them at will, as they were no longer her master, but she was theirs.

At last, brimful with excellent food and numerous glasses of delicate refreshing drinks, and exhausted by so much laughter, singing and cheering, and as it was now the early hours of the next morning, they all said their farewells and thanks to Mr Jeremiah Swan. Linked by arms, wings and paws, they slowly filed their way back to Waters-edge.

Soon they were all indoors and safely tucked up in bed. They all felt at peace with the world and twice as happy; they were soon fast asleep.

Deptus, though, lay awake for a while longer, staring into the darkness with his front paws tucked behind his head. Deptus was not a cat to dwell on things emotional, but he allowed himself a little self-indulgence on this night of all nights. He began to ponder about things in general and on his life in particular. He recalled the day, all that time ago, when he went on the day trip to Landsmoth and met Daxham, who had sat on the wall next to him eating his large melting ice cream stuck in a huge cornet, and how everything he had experienced since then had followed on from that unforgettable first occasion. It was, though, not long before Deptus, who was now feeling very tired, sighed deeply and, breathing in the gentle fragrance from his lavender-filled pillow, and feeling thankful for the gift of loyal and faithful friends, fell fast asleep.

Next morning Rilganna was up at her usual time to

greet the start of the new day with a new zest for life and a contented mind and when everyone was finally gathered at the large kitchen table, they had a hearty breakfast washed down by many cups of refreshing tea. As everyone had something special to recall, they spent a long time chattering, laughing, and going over the doings from the night before.

After breakfast Bardwell got busy preparing tasty snacks for their friends to eat on the coach as they soon had to make their way back to the city of Dunlace. Mr Swan had insisted that Rilganna take home the remains of the celebration cake and white chocolate truffles that they had all enjoyed the night before, and so she placed substantial portions in a tin for Deptus to deliver to Burgatus, Belltring and Albert.

By twelve noon the city visitors and Deptus were all packed up and ready to leave, but their hearts were resting heavily at the thought of parting from everyone at Waters-edge as their lives had become intertwined with an affection that was as solid as a rock-face. As all good things must come to an end, sadly their departure could no longer be delayed, and it was time to leave; all from Waters-edge accompanied Deptus and the visitors to the coach station. No one wanted to say farewell but after repeated and protracted hugs all round the coach driver insisted that he had to get going, and as the coach disappeared down the road the Waters-edge residents waved and waved until their arms ached and the coach was finally out of sight.

Bardwell, Peckleton, Rilganna, Daxham and Zig-Zag Pontoon, managing to swallow their tears, linked wings, arms, and paws and reminded themselves how very tasty

Bardwell's newly bottled raspberry jam would be on some tasty scones, washed down by cups of minty tea, and just as if a sudden gale had caught them in their stride they hurried as fast as they could go all the way back to Waters-edge.

28

The Temporary Farewell

Matt's project was now all but over. It had taken several weeks, and he had worked on it all day, every day. Having looked back over as much of his work as he could cope with in one go, he shut down his machine, got up from the table and tidily pushed his chair underneath. As he slowly turned to leave the room, he was stopped dead in his tracks.

He stared in disbelief, for there in the corner of the room was Bardwell; he was standing with Deptus by his side, and there, a little further away from them, was a plump, smartly dressed puffin wearing a yellow dinner jacket and bright orange cravat, whose image began to slowly fade away.

Bardwell and Deptus were earnestly chatting together as they always did, as if there was not a minute to waste. Deptus must have just arrived from the city of Dunlace for his usual weekend stay at Waters-edge, as he was carrying a tin. Matt had no doubt that it contained a large fruit cake, no doubt similar to the one that Belltring often sent along with Deptus to give to Rilganna as a treat for their tea at the weekend.

Matt gulped and involuntarily shook his head; tears began to sting his eyes and obstruct his vision as he stared in front of him. He was panic-stricken. He wanted to call out, 'Hello, over here; it's me,' but he was afraid to move lest he frighten the characters away. He felt a deep attachment for them, far deeper than he had ever experienced for anything or anyone else before. It was a couple of minutes before the precious images of Bardwell and Deptus began to fade away. Matt hurried over to where they had been standing and cried out, 'Come back, here I am; I miss you all. I want to thank you for being my companions and for sharing your life with me throughout my illness.'

Matt stopped in his tracks, as he felt that he must not fear for his own reason, but he couldn't control his agonised mind as it continued to churn over and over what he had seen. He so desperately wanted to know whether Bardwell and Deptus had been aware of his presence.

Ill at ease, he went up to bed early, turned out the light and, behaving like an insecure child, he curled his legs upwards towards his chin and tightly closed his eyes, so desperate was he for the relief of sleep.

Waking up early the next morning, Matt found his mobile phone was "purring" and an oddly worded text message was telling him to go to his computer. It didn't make any sense to him, and as he could find no trace of the sender, he deleted it.

After a morning breakfast snack, he went back to his workroom and turned on his laptop in the normal way and waited for it to activate. He was miserable, and so decided to get on with some work early, to try to engage his mind in a purposeful way. Instead of the computer behaving normally the screen turned deep purple and shuddered quite severely. Then across the screen in emboldened white lettering came the following message:

Things are well with us here, we are safe. We send you our good wishes from all at Waters-edge and Fremont House. We promise to keep you updated with all our news. This is all for now.

Was it that his whole body had been hit by an avalanche? That's what it felt like. He stood up and let the edge of the table support his stooping frame.

For a moment he began to wonder if he had seen what he had seen!

There was no option to reply and no way to save the precious message that was gradually fading but Matt knew that the connection was real enough. He felt such overwhelming joy. He now understood what it must feel like to be miraculously saved from drowning by a friend and to be forever grateful; what's more, he was confident that he was completely sane and still connected to the world that he had become so engaged with and attached to. He would patiently wait for more news for as long as it took.

It was now an existence worth living but for the moment he had no idea what a vital part of a complicated jigsaw he would become.

Meanwhile observers of the experiment undertaken by Kettlebaston, Meynell and Jasper landed safely back to Earth.

As is customary on these occasions they could recall nothing of their experiences upon their return. This was necessary to prevent them from talking to others about sensitive material. As and when appropriate their memory would be rewound and they would be debriefed.

This is all for now.